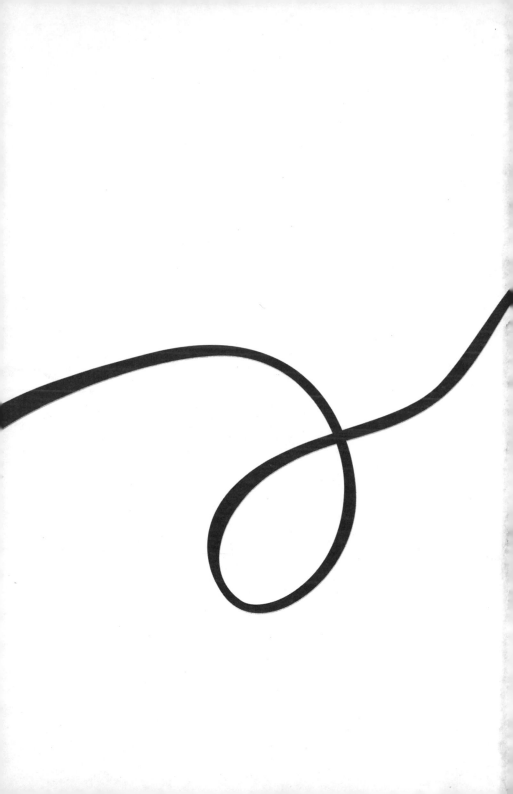

the time-traveling fashionista

a novel by

BIANCA TURETSKY

poppy

LITTLE, BROWN AND COMPANY
NEW YORK BOSTON

Poppy

Hachette Book Group
237 Park Avenue, New York, NY 10017
For more of your favorite books, visit our website at www.pickapoppy.com

Poppy is an imprint of Little, Brown and Company.
The Poppy name and logo are trademarks of Hachette Book Group, Inc.

The publisher is not responsible for websites (or their contents) that are not owned by the publisher.

First Edition: April 2011

This book is a work of historical fiction. In order to give a sense of the times, the names of certain real historical people, places, and events have been included in the book, but are used fictitiously. The non-historical characters and events portrayed in this book are the product of the author's imagination. Any similarity of such non-historical persons or events to real ones is purely coincidental.

ISBN 978-0-316-10542-2

10 9 8 7 6 5 4 3 2 1

SC

Printed in China

Book design by Alison Impey

To my Grandma,
the original Louise Lambert

"A new dress doesn't get
you anywhere; it's the life
you're living in the dress and
the sort of life you had lived before,
and what you will do in it later."

DIANA VREELAND,
fashion icon and former
editor in chief, *Vogue* magazine

CHAPTER 1

The invitation arrived on an ordinary Thursday. When Louise Lambert came home from swim practice that April afternoon, as she did every Thursday afternoon, it was lying on top of a pile of mail on the antique, oak hall table. She grabbed the lavender envelope on her way upstairs.

Louise dropped her purple backpack haphazardly in the middle of her room and flopped down on her full-size canopy bed to examine the letter. The envelope was addressed with her name.

To: Ms. Louise Lambert

Her name was written in a beautiful, sweeping script. There was no street address, no return address, and no stamp. She turned over the envelope; it was sealed with blood-red wax, a strange and old fashioned touch.

Louise rarely received any mail aside from her monthly *Teen Vogue*, Anthropologie catalog, and an occasional Hallmark card, with a twenty-dollar bill enclosed, from Grandpa Leo in Florida. She took an extra moment opening this one, feeling the weight and texture of the paper, examining the seal like a scientist. It seemed to be a monogram of the letters *MLG*, intertwined like vines. Her impatience and curiosity prevailed, and she ripped open the envelope, breaking the thick seal.

Cool! And what perfect timing. Maybe she would find a fabulous dress for the seventh-grade semiformal next Friday.

Her first dance. Louise twirled around her room with an imaginary partner as though dancing in a fancy ballroom, stopping abruptly in front of the full-length mirror that hung on the back of her door.

The mirror was covered in taped-up photographs of fashion models she'd ripped out of *Teen Vogue*, overlapped with pictures of Old Hollywood movie stars like Marilyn Monroe and Elizabeth Taylor she had printed from the Internet.

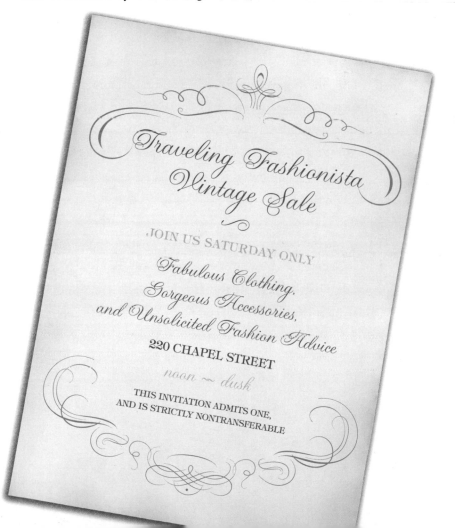

Traveling Fashionista Vintage Sale

JOIN US SATURDAY ONLY

Fabulous Clothing,
Gorgeous Accessories,
and Unsolicited Fashion Advice

220 CHAPEL STREET

noon ~ dusk

THIS INVITATION ADMITS ONE,
AND IS STRICTLY NONTRANSFERABLE

Growing up in England, Louise's mom always loved Old Hollywood movies, and said that was the reason she moved to the States as a young woman. She thought life in America must be like a classic movie, as magical as *The Wizard of Oz* and as romantic as *Casablanca*. Louise had inherited her mom's love of the Golden Age of Cinema, and some of her favorite memories involved curling up on the couch with her mom and a bowl of microwave popcorn, watching black-and-white classics with Cary Grant, the George Clooney of his day, or Audrey Hepburn on the television screen.

Louise studied her reflection and was once again disappointed. She was still short, still had braces, and, she saw as she turned to the side, was still flat as a board. Her shoulder-length, curly brown hair, damp from swim practice, was pulled into a tight little bun at the nape of her neck, with a few frizzies escaping around her face.

She picked up her antique Polaroid camera, pressed the automatic timer, and waited. Five...four...three...two... FLASH. The camera spit out an underdeveloped picture, and Louise labeled it *April 14* with a ballpoint pen. She placed it with all the others, in the top drawer of her dresser under her balled-up socks and underwear, not waiting for it to come into focus. One day she was sure she would see a change. Something. She was waiting for something to be different.

CHAPTER 2

Louise had almost thirty minutes until dinner. Bored, she restlessly pushed open her closet door and stepped into the musty annex. Her closet was huge—about half the size of her bedroom. But because of the house's steep gabled roof, the ceiling slanted sharply and rendered half the space useless. One bare bulb illuminated the room with a dim, shadowy glow. Her vast walk-in closet was by far her favorite hideout in the huge, drafty house. It was the only place left where she still felt the nervous anticipation that extraordinary and magical things could happen if she let her imagination go wild. She wasn't a kid anymore, though, so she couldn't help feeling a little self-conscious now at her excitement over a closet.

When Louise was younger, she liked building forts in here; it was cozy and dark and somehow made her feel safe. She spent hours reading with a flashlight in the nest of blankets she would arrange for just this purpose. Over the past year, as her interest in fashion grew exponentially from the J.Crew catalog to Rodarte (the only dress she owned by them was made for Target, but still, an actual designer label), she realized how lucky she was to have such a great storage area entirely for her clothing. It was one of the lucky breaks of being an only child.

Her enthusiasm was sparked by a visit about a year ago to a thrift store on the Lower East Side of New York City with her best friend, Brooke. Louise bought an amazing, one-of-a-kind, colorful knit dress that, according to the salesgirl, looked like a classic Missoni piece from the 1970s. She wore it to Caroline Epstein's bat mitzvah. The dress got her a million compliments and cost her only $13.50. She was hooked.

A suspended wooden bar spanning the length of the closet hung from the highest point of the sloped ceiling. Her father, in a surprising burst of do-it-yourself fervor, had constructed it for her last year out of some rope and dowels to house what she had hoped would be an increasingly expansive collection. At this moment, her vintage acquisitions weren't much of a collection at all. They were more like three random pieces. But she was hoping that soon things would change.

Now she loved vintage fashion. If she couldn't live in an old movie, at least she could dress the part. That was where she and her mom differed. Her mom thought films should be old, but clothes should be new and donated to, not purchased at, places like the Salvation Army.

When Louise wasn't scouring the two local thrift stores, she was online researching different designers and eras. A well-worn copy of *Shopping for Vintage: The Definitive Guide to Fashion*, a surprisingly perfect birthday gift from Grandpa Leo, was conveniently placed on her bedside table, so that if she dreamed of a particular outfit, which Louise often did, she could look it up before it disappeared from her mind's eye. The book also gave her lots of tips for collecting vintage, and a directory of all of the best vintage stores throughout the world. She would read through the shop listings on nights when she couldn't fall asleep. Names like Decades, The Diva's Closet, and Polka Dots and Moonbeams. They all sounded so alluring! It was much more effective than counting sheep.

Louise now considered herself somewhat of an expert on vintage clothing. She could easily tell a Balenciaga from a Givenchy. She knew that the term "vintage" referred to clothing up until the early 1980s, and everything past that would just be considered secondhand. She could tell a Coco Chanel suit from a Karl Lagerfeld suit for Chanel. (Current Chanel designer Karl's skirt would fall above the knee—House of Chanel founder Coco would have found that indecent.) She knew that zippers were rarely used before the 1940s. And she also knew that just because something was old, it wasn't necessarily valuable.

Louise pulled out a royal blue, knee-length flapper dress

with a drop waist, sequins, and ostrich-feather trim, from her 1920s section (presently rather limited to this one piece). It wasn't a genuine Madeleine Vionnet, the French fashion designer of the twenties and thirties who basically invented the bias cut, but on her current allowance, it was about as close as she was going to get. Noting that a matching sapphire boa and T-strap heels would perfectly complete the look, Louise remembered the invitation to the Traveling Fashionista Vintage Sale.

That would be a great place to look, she thought, excited about the prospect of adding to her collection. At this point, she had completely exhausted the local Salvation Army and Goodwill stores.

Hugging the flapper dress to her body, Louise closed her eyes and stopped for a moment to lose herself in the fantasy of the outfit. It almost felt *real.* She was dancing in a speakeasy. It was loud and sweaty, and she swayed to the imaginary jazz music playing in her head and twirled an invisible string of pearls between her fingers.

"Louise! Supper is ready!" Her mother's shrill voice permeated her consciousness.

What an exciting life the woman who owned this dress must have led! Going to parties wearing this fabulous sparkling garment—Louise guessed it was most likely a life of dancing in secret backroom joints, gambling, and gangsters.

She had read about the Roaring Twenties in history last year. The farthest Louise had gone dressed in this outfit was in front of her bedroom mirror. She was excited for the dance because now she actually had an opportunity to dress up for something besides her own fashion shoots with her Polaroid.

"Louise! I mean it!"

Well, for one thing, she bet this woman's life hadn't involved a nagging mother who freaked out if she was five minutes late for dinner.

CHAPTER 3

The Lamberts always ate dinner in the formal dining room. They lived in a large, rambling Tudor home, with lots of rooms that always needed dusting, a back staircase, dumbwaiter, and two guest bedrooms whose doors remained closed. For a family of three, it was enormous, but Louise knew every inch of it by heart—every squeaky floorboard and reading nook, and all the best spots for hide-and-seek. It was the kind of place that felt like there had to be a secret passageway somewhere, and Louise was still determined to find it.

Often it was only she and her mother sitting around the long mahogany table. Dark and shadowy oil portraits of Louise's ancestors hung gloomily on the Venetian red walls. Her father rarely made it home for supper, often working late hours at his law firm. Dinnertime was when she most wished she had brothers and sisters to talk to. Sometimes she would imagine that her two-dimensional painted relatives climbed out of their canvas backgrounds and sat around the long table with Louise and her mom, filling the room with laughter and lively conversations about her family's history.

Mrs. Lambert was already at the head of the table when Louise came down. "Dahling, what were you doing up there? The meat is getting cold," she said in her faintly accented English, unfolding the white linen napkin and placing it on her lap.

"Sorry, Mom, I guess I got a little distracted," Louise said, plunking down into the uncomfortable high-back chair.

"Hmm." Mrs. Lambert sighed. "Why am I not surprised?" she asked, daintily cutting up a gray piece of mystery meat.

Before moving to Connecticut, her mother had grown up in a wealthy family in London and, unfortunately for Louise, after a lifetime of maid service, Mrs. Lambert never really learned to cook. Boiled sausages, boiled potatoes, boiled peas and carrots. It was always some variation of this bland, over-cooked food that her mother drenched in malt vinegar. Mrs. Lambert insisted that dousing every bite in vinegar was a typically English way to eat, which may have been the case, but it still tasted pretty awful. She wished they could eat a normal dinner like macaroni and cheese at the kitchen counter or pepperoni pizza in front of the television like everyone else got to. Whenever a friend came over for supper, Louise couldn't help but be a little embarrassed by their formality.

"Did you see that letter for you on the hall table?" Mrs. Lambert asked.

Louise nodded, her mouth full of mush.

"What was it? Another bat mitzvah?"

"No, an invitation to a vintage sale this Saturday. It looks cool. I thought I could get a dress for the dance," Louise said eagerly.

"Used clothes? Personally, dahling, I don't know why you can't buy a new dress. We can go shopping together this weekend if you'd like. The owners of those clothes are probably dead by now. Their belongings sold off in an estate sale," Mrs. Lambert said. She gave a dramatic shudder, clearly not pleased with Louise's new shopping habits.

"Mom, they're just vintage clothes! And they're special, one-of-a-kind," she explained. Louise didn't understand why her mom didn't get it.

"Do as you like, dear. I'm just saying that I'll be more than happy to give you money for a new dress. Isn't that what the other girls will be wearing?"

Louise and Mrs. Lambert returned to eating their boiled mush in silence. The only sound was the clinking of the silver cutlery against the china.

"Mom, tell me again about Aunt Alice?" Louise asked, staring up at the portrait of her great-aunt hanging on the wall behind her mother's head.

Mrs. Lambert had flown to London last week for Alice's daughter's funeral. Louise had wanted to go. She looked for any excuse to travel, even the funeral of a distant second cousin who she had met only once before. Her mother never liked her to miss school, so Louise stayed home with her dad.

She loved hearing stories about her mother's family. Her mom was naturally a bit dramatic and therefore was a gifted storyteller.

"Well, dahling, when my aunt Alice was younger, she was a great beauty, and a talented actress," Mrs. Lambert started.

Louise looked up again at the old lady with a face like a French poodle suspended in the dusty, ornate frame.

"Really?" Louise asked, incredulous. She had heard bits of this story before, but it was still difficult to reconcile that image in the painting with anyone under the age of ninety. She would have to take her mom's word for that.

"Yes, it's true. She was quite famous back in her day."

"She sounds so cool. I wish I'd met her."

"She was certainly a character," Mrs. Lambert said with a sigh. "Her life definitely could have been made into a movie. Even I didn't know the whole truth until last week."

"What do you mean?" Louise asked, curious that someone in her family had lived a film-worthy life. Her reverie was interrupted by the sound of a distant, ringing phone line from her bedroom.

Mrs. Lambert stared off into space, lost in her own thoughts. She had that dreamer's ability to completely lose herself in her own head, much like Louise. "That, my dear, will have to wait until you are a bit older."

"Well, may I be excused, then?" Louise asked, shrugging off that her mother didn't think she was old enough to hear about her own family. "That was probably Brooke calling. We have a ton of math homework tonight."

Louise cleared the table and ran up to her room to call her best friend so they could finish their assignment together over the phone. Mrs. Lambert washed the dishes.

It seemed to be just an ordinary Thursday.

CHAPTER 4

"I'm afraid Kip isn't going to ask! What is he waiting for?" Brooke said with a groan from the other end of the phone line. "I mean the dance is in, like, *less* than a week."

Louise could picture Brooke in her bedroom, painting her toenails while watching television and balancing her math book on her lap. She always had to be doing at least three things at once. Louise heard sitcom laughter in the background.

"He'll ask," Louise assured her. "But what about me? At least you have two prospects." She twirled the tangled, red phone cord around her index and middle fingers.

Mrs. Lambert was convinced that talking on a cell phone would immediately result in brain cancer, so her parents had a private phone line installed in Louise's room. Her phone was shaped like an oversized pair of lips, a replica of something she had seen in a cheesy eighties movie that she had bought on eBay.

"I bet Todd Berkowitz will ask you," Brooke teased.

Louise rolled her eyes. Todd was, well, Todd. First of all, he was as tall as Louise, in other words, not very tall. Kind of pimply, although this year Louise noticed he seemed to find the right dose of Proactiv. He was always wearing a hoodie and jeans that were ten sizes too big, and he rode his beloved skateboard constantly, even in the school hallways, much to the annoyance of the teachers. Louise was pretty sure Todd had a major crush on her for the past year and that everyone knew it. She was both kind of excited and totally embarrassed at the same time, since he was the first guy she knew of who liked her. She supposed he was slightly cute, at least compared to the other guys at her middle school. But compared with the movie stars she idolized, Todd fell pretty short—literally.

He wasn't at all who Louise dreamed would be her date to the dance or her first kiss. In the movies in her head, she imagined someone taller, with broader shoulders, more classically handsome and rugged, and, well, kind of in black-and-white. Like James Dean in the old film *Rebel Without a Cause*. The reality of her life was totally disappointing in comparison.

She walked over to her goldfish, Marlon, and dropped a few orange flakes into the glass bowl. That was about as close as she was going to get to Marlon Brando, perhaps the greatest movie actor of all time, star of such classics as *On the Waterfront* and *A Streetcar Named Desire*. A goldfish.

When she thought about it, she realized the films she watched with her mom sometimes seemed more real to her than her actual life.

"Can we please change the subject?" Louise asked in response. "It's too disturbing."

"Lou, you are so dramatic. Wait, what am I going to do about Kip?"

Louise shook her head. Talk about drama. "So do you know the answer to number six?"

That night Louise dreamed she was at the dance. She knew it was the seventh-grade semiformal, but nothing looked quite right. The gymnasium had turned into a grand ballroom, and all the faces of the people dancing were weirdly familiar but also strangely different at the same time. They kind of looked like her friends, but they weren't. Suddenly Louise realized she must be at the wrong party. Just then she saw a guy in a black hooded sweatshirt ride past her on a skateboard. She ran after him, calling Todd's name, thinking he'd be able to show her where to go, but he didn't turn around. It was like she wasn't even there.

Louise bolted upright in bed. She looked over at her clock radio: the red glowing lights spelled out 2:20 AM. Why was she having so much anxiety about this dance? Who was she kidding? All she could think about was the dance! She tossed and turned for the rest of the night. Louise had slept for only five hours when her alarm woke her at 7:17 that morning for another school day.

Louise rolled out of bed. She changed out of her soft, cotton, oversized Gap nightshirt into her favorite, vintage, lavender cashmere sweater, with only one tiny moth hole on the elbow, her perfectly broken-in Levi's, and neon pink Converse sneakers. She pulled her hair tightly back in an elastic-secured bun, not letting any curls escape.

She snapped another Polaroid, labeled it *April 15,* and watched the gray film slowly dissolve into focus. Nothing. No changes, except for two dark rings under her eyes that gave her face a haunted expression. The day had hardly begun, and she was already exhausted.

Like every morning, she ripped off a page on her daily Virgo horoscope calendar hoping for some exciting predictions: "You will embark on an interesting voyage. Stay true to yourself and enjoy the adventure!"—maybe she'd get asked out on her voyage to school? The bus would be arriving in twenty minutes.

"Good morning, dear," Mrs. Lambert cheerfully greeted Louise, in a tone that was remarkably chipper for that time of day.

Louise's mom insisted that her daughter eat breakfast each morning, and she was vigorously stirring a clad-iron pot on the stove with a wooden spoon when Louise shuffled into the

stately old kitchen. Louise was never hungry at 7:30 AM, and each bite of oatmeal was its own special torture.

"Morning," she mumbled as she took her seat at the breakfast nook and began to absentmindedly poke at her fruit plate with a fork. Her father was already at the table, dressed in his pressed Brooks Brothers suit and striped tie, drinking coffee and reading the *New York Times*. If you looked up "lawyer" in the dictionary, there was probably a picture of Robert Lambert, with his neatly trimmed salt-and-pepper hair and wire-rimmed glasses. He just looked the part.

"Good morning, chicken," he said, glancing up briefly from his paper. Louise had no idea how that nickname started, but somehow, to her bewilderment, it stuck.

"Eating breakfast every day is good for your memory," Mrs. Lambert explained yet again as she noticed Louise gagging on a piece of cantaloupe. "They've done studies." Mrs. Lambert liked to justify all her unjustified rules with "they've done studies." Who "they" were Louise had no idea, and she was pretty sure her mother didn't, either.

"I know, I know," Louise said. "With all the breakfasts I've eaten by now, I'll be remembering things that have never even happened." She moaned audibly, not sure how she was going to manage another bite.

"Don't be smart with me, young lady," Mrs. Lambert retorted, a little smile cracking through her tough façade.

"Okay, good enough," she decided, wiping her hands on her apron. "Go get your books. You don't want to miss the bus again."

Louise sat at the table for another moment, too full and sleepy to move.

"And if your memory is so sharp," her mother continued, "you will recall my taxi rates have gone up. I now charge ten dollars for a school drop."

Her daughter bolted from the kitchen.

CHAPTER 5

"Class, do you know what day it is today?" Miss Morris asked the sea of expressionless faces. Miss Morris had been teaching at Fairview Junior High for eons; even Louise's father had suffered through her history classes. Everyone was pretty sure that she hadn't changed her lesson plans since then. She was a tiny old lady with legs as thin as Number Two pencils and a tight white bun that never a stray hair escaped from.

"Anyone?" she asked in a tone that revealed she had given up hope of her students answering her years ago.

Silence. *Click. Click. Click.* Louise never realized how loud these institutional school clocks actually were until she had Miss Morris for history.

"Today is exactly one year from *the one-hundredth anniversary* of the RMS *Titanic* disaster." Miss Morris paused for a dramatic moment, or to catch her breath, and waited for some reaction. She was wearing a steel gray, boiled-wool dress that looked extremely itchy and hot for this time of year. Apparently Miss Morris's wardrobe was not affected by the change of seasons.

Click. Click. Click.

She was probably old enough to have been on the *Titanic* herself, Louise thought, already bored. Miss Morris had an uncanny ability to make even the most interesting subject matter as dull as a Lambert meatloaf recipe.

"Can anyone tell me anything about the *Titanic*?"

"The movie blew," Billy Robertson said from his seat at the back of the classroom. Miss Morris ignored him, or perhaps didn't hear. Louise could never be sure, but Miss Morris never reacted to Billy's sarcastic remarks.

"The *Titanic* was by far the most luxurious ship to ever cross the ocean," the white-bunned teacher began in her monotone, though by the somewhat sparkly look in her otherwise cloudy brown eyes, she seemed to at least be entertaining herself. "She was the largest passenger steamship in the world at the time of her sinking."

Louise looked around at the rest of her fidgety classmates. Mostly everyone had already tuned out, so she focused her attention on sketching fantasy dress designs in her loose-leaf notebook. This came to be a problem before every test when she'd open her notepad, praying that miraculously there would be some actual notes, and would inevitably find a sketchbook that would be useful only to someone studying for an entrance exam at the Fashion Institute of Technology.

What were they wearing on the Titanic? Louise wondered, and without overthinking, she let her wrist relax and started drawing what she imagined was the fashion at the time. She sketched a long, softly draped ankle-length skirt with a high, empire waist and intricate lace detailing. The skirt was wide at the hips and got narrower toward the feet. She drew a pair of high, slightly curved heels with straps crisscrossing at the ankles, peeking out of the hem. A beautiful lace blouse with a modest neckline sat below a hat with a wide, face-shadowing brim so she didn't have to draw the facial features. Louise wasn't sure where she got the idea or how historically accurate it was, but on closer examination, she smiled, satisfied with how it turned out.

She was abruptly awoken from her dress-designing day-dream when the bell rang and announced the end of another forgettable history class.

CHAPTER 6

By the time Louise realized that Todd Berkowitz was waiting for her outside of the classroom, it was too late. Did he have her schedule memorized or something? Wasn't that considered stalking in some states? When she stepped out into the crowded hallway in a Miss Morris–induced stupor, he rushed over to her and accidentally knocked her books out of her hands.

Louise watched in seeming slow motion as the sketches she had just been working on fell out of her notebook and scattered on the puke green linoleum tiled floor.

"Sorry, Louise," Todd croaked, his face turning as crimson as his oversized red polo shirt. He knelt down to pick up the collateral damage.

"Cool, these are really good," he said, examining the drawings.

Louise scrambled to hide the images on the loose-leaf paper; she wasn't ready to show them to anyone yet.

"Oh, thanks," she mumbled. "They're not finished."

"So anyway," he started, getting to his feet. "I was just thinking, maybe if you weren't, you know, like, going with anyone to the dance..." He trailed off, nervously spinning the wheel of his skateboard.

Was that a question? Louise waited. She looked at him and didn't want to be able to look him directly in the eye. She wanted him to be taller.

"You know, maybe we can carpool together or whatever. Save the environment."

Carpool together or whatever? How am I supposed to respond to that? I don't know what to do!

For some inexplicable reason, the only thing she could think of suddenly was to walk as fast as she could in the opposite direction without uttering a single word. Halfway down the hall, she looked back over her shoulder and saw Todd shake his head in confusion, get on his skateboard, and ride off in the other direction, almost taking down Miss Morris in the process.

Louise let out a long breath, and then sighed again.

CHAPTER 7

"Louise? Louise, are you even listening to me?" Brooke asked in an annoyed tone.

Louise was standing in front of her closed locker, absentmindedly spinning the dial of her combination lock, completely lost in her own thoughts, imagining she was blonde fifties movie icon Marilyn Monroe, wearing that iconic white halter dress at a fabulous Hollywood party. Daydreams were the only way she could get through another day that seemed exactly like the previous one at Fairview Junior High.

"Sorry, what did you say?" Louise snapped back to reality, Marilyn's image instantly transformed into the pretty, familiar face of her best friend.

"I said," Brooke repeated, "Michael just asked me to the dance. But I don't want to say yes, because what if Kip asks me?"

Louise rolled her eyes. This was a typical problem for

Brooke. She was naturally, genetically blessed model thin, with dirty-blonde hair that cascaded halfway down her back in perfect, frizzless waves, wide, pale blue eyes, and a cherry red pout. Kind of like Marilyn Monroe, if Marilyn were into Juicy Couture and seriously anorexic.

In other words, Brooke Patterson was very popular. She also happened to be Louise's best friend, due mostly to the fact that they had been friends since they were practically babies. Their fathers had been in the same fraternity in college and now worked at the same law firm. Louise secretly hoped that she and Brooke would end up like that someday, best friends, with their kids being best friends, too.

"I think you should just say you'll think about it, and then if Kip asks you by tomorrow you can still go with him," Louise rationalized. Somehow giving advice to her friends was easy, but in her own life, she did ridiculous and embarrassing things like running away from the one guy who was trying to ask her to the dance. She was too mortified to even talk about it with Brooke yet. "Keep your options open a little longer."

"Right, good idea," Brooke replied and grinned. "So what are you going to wear?"

"I don't know yet." Louise pulled out the Fashionista Vintage Sale invite from her backpack and handed it to her best friend. "Maybe I'll find something here."

Now it was Brooke's turn to roll her eyes. "Louise, why don't you come to the mall with me after school? We can get something normal. I think Nordstrom just got a shipment of Marc Jacobs. I mean it's like you're permanently trapped in another era. It *is* 2011, you know."

Louise had finally freed the combination lock and opened her locker.

"See? I rest my case." Brooke sighed. Louise's locker was decorated much like her bedroom at home. Black-and-white photographs of a young Faye Dunaway and Warren Beatty from the set of the chic gangster movie *Bonnie and Clyde*, and Twiggy, the Kate Moss of the 1960s, smiled back at her from the inside of the metal door. They were a little reminder to her that there was more to life than junior high, and that a more glamorous world was waiting for her somewhere out there, even if it was just in her imagination at this point.

Louise felt her cheeks get a little flushed. Maybe it was a bit pathetic. Maybe she should wake up and start living in the twenty-first century.

"But that's why I love you and all of your quirky charm." Brooke gave Louise a quick hug. "See you on the bus," she called over her shoulder. "I'm late for earth science review."

As she bounced down the hallway, Louise was left alone staring at her time capsule of a locker.

The rest of the school day dragged on, as Friday afternoon classes tended to do. Louise showed the vintage sale invitation to a few of her friends in eighth-period English lit class. She was curious if anyone else had received an invite in the mail. Strangely enough, she seemed to be the only one.

CHAPTER 8

Louise and Brooke were both a bit mortified by the fact that they still had to take the bus in the seventh grade, but at least they were on the same bus route.

"Do you ever wish you were someone else?" Louise asked, flipping through a dog-eared copy of *Us Weekly*. The bus was loud and crowded with hyperactive sixth graders, and a few unlucky kids from seventh and eighth. Brooke and Louise always sat together in the same seat on the left, three back from the front, and everyone on the bus knew better than to sit there. That little show of respect and seniority was the only redeeming feature of their otherwise torturous ride.

"No, not really," Brooke replied honestly. "God, what is she wearing?" she asked, peering over Louise's shoulder as she flipped past a photo of Renée Zellweger in baggy sweatpants and Uggs waiting in line at the supermarket.

"There's no magic anymore," Louise said with a sigh. "Why

do they insist on showing everyone that 'Stars Are Just Like Us'? I liked it better when you could imagine they weren't. Like they woke up looking fabulous."

"And their morning breath smells like strawberries," Brooke added sarcastically. "Get real, Louise. People are people."

Brooke had an open compact in one hand and was trying to apply lip gloss with the other, in between potholes. At that moment, the bus hit a particularly deep rut.

"Darn," she said and looked over at Louise. A frosted pink streak connected her lip and chin. Louise laughed.

"Well, I wish I was someone who didn't have to ride the bus," Brooke said, wiping off the gloss with a tissue.

"I don't mean someone else entirely," Louise clarified, "but more like you, but in a different life."

"Hey, Louise," Billy Robertson called from across the aisle, before Brooke had a chance to respond. Billy's mop of brown hair covered his eyes like a limp curtain so that she had to wonder how he saw anything at all. They had been in the same class since kindergarten, but for some reason this year he had singled Louise out and made it a point to be as annoying and embarrassing to her as possible.

Leave me alone, Louise silently begged. Whenever Billy said anything, especially to her, it was generally rude and obnoxious.

"Why do you always wear those old, ratty clothes? We all know you live in that big old giant house—you trying to pretend like you're poor or something?"

Louise looked down at her favorite cardigan. The tiny tear in the elbow now seemed like a gaping hole. *Why did she like vintage clothing so much?* Her life would probably be a lot easier if she at least looked like she fit in.

"Oh, shut up," Brooke responded without missing a beat. "If you knew anything about fashion—which, looking at that horrendous dirt brown sweater you wear all the time, you clearly don't—then you'd know she only wears vintage. All of the celebrities do these days," she concluded, flashing him a picture of Blake Lively photographed wearing a funky oversized magenta sweater and skinny black leggings while carrying a ginormous Starbucks coffee.

Billy looked down at the ugly, pilled pullover that he had also worn yesterday, and likely the day before, and his ears turned a hot red. "Whatever," he replied gruffly.

Brooke gave Louise's hand a quick squeeze, and Louise smiled back gratefully at her friend. "Don't worry about him. That's his caveman-like way of flirting," Brooke whispered. "I'd like to go to that Fashionista Vintage Sale with you tomorrow," she announced to Louise, throwing Billy a pointed look.

"Great!" Louise exclaimed with a smile. "Maybe we can both find old, ratty dresses for the dance."

She got off the bus at the next stop, promising to call Brooke tomorrow after lunch to make a plan to go to the mysterious sale. Hopefully, the perfect new/old dress was awaiting her.

CHAPTER 9

On Saturday, after an early morning swim practice and a quick chicken salad lunch, Louise rode her bike downtown to meet Brooke at the sale. The day was overcast and windy. She wiped the beads of sweat from her forehead with the sleeve of her dark denim jacket, and kept pedaling against the wind.

She never had to think about where to turn; her bike wheels would just turn. Fairview, Connecticut, was a typical, small suburban town, and Louise had lived there her whole life. The closest mall was three towns over; the movie theater had two screening rooms with screens the size of bedsheets and films that had basically already come out on DVD. To do anything that was even remotely interesting or cultural you had to get on the Metro-North train and ride forty-five minutes through the trees and fields into New York City.

When she was younger, she'd ride her bike through the streets trying to get lost, looking for an adventure. But she could never get lost. The town was too small. No matter how hard Louise tried, or how many hours she rode around, she always ended up at home.

The sign for Chapel Street beckoned and she leaned her bike up against an old oak tree, double-checking the address on the invitation. Number 220 Chapel Street was a nondescript brick building. Louise must have walked by it a thousand times without ever noticing it. Brooke was nowhere in sight. Maybe she had reconsidered her offer now that she wasn't defending her best friend from Billy.

There was nothing but dust and cobwebs in the showcase window, and Louise wondered if she'd fallen for some kind of hoax. From the street, the store looked closed and deserted. Perhaps the Traveling Fashionista Vintage Sale had already packed up and left town?

She decided to try the door anyway. To her amazement, it swung open with only the slightest touch, and Louise stepped hesitantly into the darkness.

CHAPTER 10

"Welcome! Welcome! Marla, we have a customer, what fun!"
A crimson-haired woman with bright poppy-colored lipstick
and a wide nose popped up from behind a rack of clothes and
led Louise by the arm into the dark, stuffy room.

"Do you have your invitation, dear?" an unidentified female
voice called from the depths of the shop. "Glenda, do check
that she has an invitation."

Louise extracted the embossed, lilac-colored invitation from
the front pocket of her backpack and presented it to Glenda.

The shop was dusty and bursting with armoires, racks of
old clothes, and tall columns of hatboxes precariously piled to
an alarming height. The woman named Marla was partially
hidden behind a mahogany rolltop desk in the back corner.
The desk was a disorganized mess, covered in papers and fabric and leather-bound books.

"Oh, wonderful," Glenda chirped as she plucked the card

from Louise's hand and, without bothering to look at it, nonchalantly tossed it over her shoulder onto the floor.

Glenda had red frizzy hair fastened in a messy chignon with black enamel chopsticks. Her dress was simple black wool, shapeless, almost monastic. She was exceptionally tall, an intimidating feature accentuated by her black Victorian lace-up boots with three-inch stacked heels.

"Please have a look around. Sorry for the clutter, but this space is temporary. We'll be moving soon," the woman named Marla announced.

She had emerged from behind the desk, small and mousy. Her stringy chestnut-colored hair fell limply to her shoulders. The one distinguishing feature adorning her unremarkable face was a wart the size of a peanut that had planted itself on the tip of her nose. Louise noticed that the two women were both wearing matching oval-framed pictures of a black poodle that hung around their necks by heavy gold chains.

Louise hated being the only customer in a store. The attention made her self-conscious as she began looking through the tightly packed racks of clothes. The two overbearing women didn't make it any more comfortable as they followed a few paces behind her, pausing when she stopped to examine a swishy powder blue dress more carefully.

Luckily, Brooke burst into the store before things got too uncomfortable.

"Sorry I'm late," she panted, looking around the room in awe or horror, Louise wasn't sure which. "Where are we?" she asked. Her eyebrows furrowed. "I never knew this existed."

"I know. It's cool, right?" Louise gushed, trying to sound enthusiastic, but already pretty sure that she would not hear the end of this.

"Dahling, do you have an invitation?" Glenda asked, giving Brooke a thorough once-over. She was wearing her weekend uniform, a blueberry-colored Juicy Couture terry tracksuit.

"She's with me," Louise said protectively.

"Well, I suppose that's fine," Marla replied, circling Brooke suspiciously.

"You suppose?" Brooke raised an eyebrow, and started looking through the clothing racks. "You owe me one," she said under her breath.

There were no prices listed on anything, and when Brooke asked about the cost of a black cocktail dress, Glenda and Marla glanced at each other with a look of surprise, as though the question of pricing had never crossed their minds.

"Well, oh dear, I don't know. One dollar. Is that reasonable?" Glenda asked, rummaging through a stack of papers on the desk.

"No, no, no. Things have changed, Glenda. Inflation, deflation, extortion. One million dollars? Is that fair?"

Louise and Brooke laughed. The black satin dress was in

the style of the 1960s. It was classic yet flirty and looked like something the famous American designer Halston would have made for Jackie O to wear at a White House dinner party. But for one million dollars, they would have to pass.

"Oops. Too much?" Marla blushed.

"Let's forget about money for now," Glenda decided. "So corrupting, so unnecessary among friends. We'll figure it out at a later date. Let's just worry about finding something pretty for your friend."

"But what about me?" Brooke asked, not used to being overlooked.

"I'm sure you'll find a nicely overpriced Marc Jacobs number at the mall later today," Glenda said and winked, much to their surprise. Wow, these ladies were good.

Glenda and Marla began rummaging through the store, unzipping garment bags, throwing unwanted items like mink stoles, wrap jersey dresses, and brightly colored silk scarves into piles on the floor. They created a cloud of dust with their excited motions. Completely caught up in their own chaos, they gave Louise and Brooke a moment of privacy to look for themselves. Louise quickly combed through the garment racks.

"Hors d'oeuvres?" Glenda asked, pronouncing the word like oars-duh-voors.

She had reappeared carrying a silver platter with a mound

of lumpy, bright orange dip. Saltine crackers were scattered around the tray. Louise looked at the food with trepidation.

"Crab dip!" Glenda announced. "Marla is absolutely famous for it."

"I'm allergic to shellfish," Brooke exclaimed, lying through her teeth. "It could, like, kill me."

Glenda pushed the platter toward Louise.

"No, thank you," Louise said politely. "I'm not really hungry. I just ate lunch."

"Oh, have a taste, dear," Marla urged. "We have very little patience for young ladies who are afraid to try new things."

Glenda gave Louise a hard, disapproving look.

"But why is it that color?" Louise asked nervously, taking a cracker and dipping it tentatively into the foreign substance. The dip had a crusty outer shell that almost broke the cracker in two, as if it had been baking all day in the sun, developing an armor to protect itself from probing crackers and girls with adventurous palettes. She didn't want to seem rude. She would just have a little.

"A generous sprinkling of sweet paprika," Marla said with a wink. "That's the secret ingredient. Don't tell."

"I won't," Louise promised. This was one secret she would be able to keep.

She popped the cracker into her mouth and chewed quickly, without breathing through her nose, and swallowed. She still tasted the creamy and fishy mush, and although she didn't like it one bit, she thanked Marla and told her that she could see why everyone loved it so much. This appeared to be one of those instances where lying was the appropriate response.

"Thank you, sweetie," Marla replied, beaming.

Marla picked a cracker from the tray and scooped out a generous amount of dip and ate it in one large bite. "Mmmm. That is truly scrumptious." She wiped the salty crumbs from her noticeable chin hairs.

"Now, please, back to shopping."

Louise carefully opened the door of an ivory-colored wardrobe that was slightly ajar. The armoire was filled with leopard print coats, high-heeled shoes, and fabulous gold-and-silver sequined gowns. A slight glimpse of iridescent pink caught her eye from the depths of the closet, and Louise pushed aside the fur coats and sparkles to get a better look.

The dress made her gasp. It was the perfect powdery pink gown, a long, draped skirt that flowed out from an empire waist, intricately detailed with shimmery gold thread and tiny silver beads. It was delicate and feminine, and Louise knew that no one at Fairview Junior High would have anything like it. She quickly plucked it out of the closet and announced that she had found *The One*.

Glenda and Marla rushed over to her, eyes gleaming, excited to see what she had picked out.

"Are you sure you want to try that one on, dear?" Marla asked Louise hesitantly.

"Of course she is," Brooke said with a nod. "Lou, that is fabulous. I mean, for vintage."

"Oh yes, I love this one," Louise cooed, pressing the cool, silky fabric to her cheek. "Please, can I try this one on?"

"What do you think, Glenda? Oh, I don't know, I just don't know...." Marla stammered, nervously playing with the poodle necklace around her neck.

"Please, I've never seen a gown like this before. It's so special."

"You have no idea, sweet pea," Glenda muttered. Her voice was husky and low—what Louise imagined was the raspy result of a lifetime of unfiltered cigarettes and too much champagne.

"Isn't this the Traveling Fashionista Vintage *Sale*?" Brooke asked. "How are you supposed to sell anything? As far as I can see, we're your only customers!"

Louise clutched the gown protectively to her chest. She wanted this dress.

"Touché. No need to be rude, princess."

Louise examined the tag in the dress to try and deduce what designer made it. The label itself was ripped out, or probably had just fallen off after decades of handling. However, the very edge of the tag was still sewn in. She could still make out the faint traces of a cursive embroidered $\mathscr{L}$.

"It even has my initial in it," she protested. "This was obviously meant for me."

The two women exchanged amused looks at Louise's persistence.

"You know, Marla, I think it would fit her marvelously. It seems like she and Miss Baxter were exactly the same size."

"Miss Baxter?" Louise questioned distractedly, her eyes drifting back to Marla's nose and that goober of a wart balancing on the tippy-tip. She wondered why Marla never had it removed. Weren't there dermatologists for that sort of thing?

"Why, that's Miss Baxter's dress, sweetie. Didn't we mention that?" Marla asked, breaking Louise's wart-induced reverie. She took the dress from the girl's arms to examine, holding it up for size.

"No, I don't believe so. Who is Miss Baxter?" Louise asked.

"Yes, yes, yes. This is just perfect. You and Miss Baxter could have been sisters. Your proportions are similar. I think she should try it on, Glenda. What do you think?"

"Oh, wait, look, it's damaged," Brooke remarked, running her thumb and forefinger along the hem. "It looks like it was torn."

"That can be fixed! A little stitch here, a stitch there. It will be as good as new. Well, not new—but it *is* vintage, you know! Yes, you must try this on." Glenda clapped her hands.

Louise held the fabric up to her nose. She cringed, looking perplexed. "It smells fishy."

"Well, nothing a little Febreze can't freshen up. Glenda, where is the Febreze?"

"It smells salty and damp, like the ocean."

"Dear, why would it smell like the ocean? You're being silly. Try it on! The color is simply divine." Marla handed Louise a flute of sparkling liquid and pushed her toward the toile-patterned changing partition.

"Loosen up! Have a cocktail—don't worry, sweetie, it's only cider. I think you're the only other person who is destined to have this dress," Glenda encouraged.

"And don't you have a dance next week?" Marla piped in.

"Umm, yes. But how did you know that?"

Louise let herself be pushed by Marla behind the partition. Her excitement at finding the perfect seventh-grade-dance dress had turned into something a bit more nerve-racking. She slowly began unlacing her dirty Converse sneakers, the nervous feeling in the pit of her stomach making an audible rumble.

"Dear, is everything all right in there?" Glenda called from the other side of the Japanese screen. "Do you need help?

Marla can button you up. She used to be the personal dresser and stylist for all of the big starlets. Louise Brooks would simply not get dressed without her."

"Who?" Louise asked.

"Nothing, dear. Come out and show us!"

"I'll be out in a minute." Louise took a gulp of the sweet sparkly liquid to calm her churning stomach and felt the bubbles go straight to her head.

"Are you sure this is only cider?"

"Ha, ha, ha. Of course, sweetie," Marla reassured her.

Louise took off her jean jacket, pulled her navy and white polka-dotted sundress over her head, and stood for a long minute in her camisole and socks on the cool hardwood floor. She slowly pulled the garment off of the wooden hanger and held the dress in front of her body while she looked at her image in the dusty and cracked mirror.

The dress was the perfect shade of pink: cotton candy, bubble gum, and Marilyn Monroe. She felt like she looked truly beautiful. She smiled a great, big, open smile, and saw reflected back at her a mouth crammed full of shiny metal braces, abruptly grounding her in the depressing reality that was her twelve-year-old life.

With a sigh, Louise picked up the pink dress and pushed her arms through the puckered sleeves and let it fall over her body like a curtain. She heard the swishing of the fabric as it slid down around her, she felt the soft silk and the itchy taf-feta netting brush against her skin, and as soon as the garment had moved into place she felt light-headed, spinning, dizzy... and then everything went black. Louise crumpled, unconscious, to the floor on a pillow of rose-colored silk.

"I don't understand how a woman can leave the house without fixing herself up a little —if only out of politeness. And then, you never know, maybe that's the day she has a date with destiny. And it's best to be as pretty as possible for destiny."

COCO CHANEL, legendary
French fashion designer

CHAPTER 11

"Miss Baxter. Miss Baxter. Wake up, Miss Baxter."

Louise opened her eyes. Her eyelids were crusted together as if after a long night's sleep. Her head was pounding, and her mouth felt like it was filled with bitter-tasting cotton balls.

"She's awake! Wow, Miss Baxter, you gave us all a scare!"

A bright light blinded Louise, and she immediately closed her eyes again. Her head was killing her, the ground was spinning, and why did it sound like this man's voice was calling her Miss Baxter? She needed to stop the spinning feeling in her head. Where was she? Louise tried to concentrate. She felt a cool breeze; the air smelled fresh and briny.

"Miss Baxter? Please open your eyes again, have a sip of water."

Louise obeyed the voice. She was looking up at an unfamiliar man with salt-and-pepper hair, a full white beard, and rosy cheeks. He was hovering over her, fanning her face with a newspaper. A man holding an old-fashioned camera with a big flash was standing alongside him. Behind them was a crowd of concerned faces, framed by an expansive bright blue sky.

"Miss Baxter, you gave us quite a scare for a minute there," the strange man said again, in what Louise detected was a British accent. He was wearing a white, buttoned-up uniform with gold braiding.

"Are we . . . are we moving?" Louise asked. She felt like she was lying on something hard and splintery.

"Well, I should hope so," he replied with a chuckle. "If we're ever to make it to New York City."

"New York City?"

"Yes, we're on our way to New York City. Don't you remember, Miss Baxter?" he asked.

"Please stop calling me that," Louise pleaded. "Who is Miss Baxter?"

The uniformed man whistled. "This is worse than I thought." He once again offered Louise a glass of water and continued fanning her with the folded newspaper. Louise accepted the drink, hoping to wash out the unpleasant taste that coated her parched mouth.

"*You* are Miss Baxter, Miss Baxter," he replied cheerfully.

Louise thought that if he said that name one more time, she would scream.

"And who are you?" she asked, completely baffled.

"Well, there, Miss Baxter. You don't remember me, either, do you?"

Louise shook her head. No, she most certainly did not.

"I'm Edward Smith." He pointed to his gold nameplate. "I'm the captain of this ship."

"We're on a ship?" she asked. The rocking motion started to make a bit more sense.

"Yes, ma'am," he replied matter-of-factly. "We left England this morning. Mr. Miller had just taken a group photograph for the *Times*, and as soon as the flash went off, you collapsed here on the A Deck. The bright light must have startled you."

"England?" Louise repeated incredulously. She must be dreaming. That was the only logical explanation.

"Yes, Miss Baxter. Don't worry, though; we'll be picking up Mr. Baxter at the next port in Cherbourg, France." *Omigod! There was a* Mr. *Baxter?!* This was worse than she thought. She needed to wake up now. Louise closed her eyes tightly and pinched herself, hard, on her right arm. It hurt.

Looking down, she saw that she was lying on a slatted wooden deck chair. She was wearing a pink evening gown and no shoes; her painted red toenails peeked out from under the fabric. Louise tried to prop herself up, becoming a bit self-conscious about the small crowd staring at her.

"Please don't move, ma'am. We don't want any more fainting spells. And I don't want you to cut yourself on the broken glass," the captain said, gesturing to the floor next to Louise's chaise. "William! Get someone to clean up this glass immediately."

"Yes, sir," a voice from the crowd answered.

Louise glanced to her left and saw a shattered champagne flute in pieces on the blond wood deck.

"William will help you back to your stateroom just as soon as you feel strong enough." The captain nodded with authority. "I must get back to my post."

"Ummm… Thanks… Captain…" Louise whispered, squinting her eyes to try and make out the name, which she had already forgotten, on his polished shiny nameplate.

EDWARD JOHN SMITH
CAPTAIN
WHITE STAR LINE

Confused, Louise grabbed the newspaper from the captain's hands and unfolded it to the front page.

The Times of London

APRIL 12, 1912

And with that news, she promptly fainted once again.

CHAPTER 12

Louise felt like she was nestled in a cloud, wrapped in something delicate and silky, and she didn't want to open her eyes and end this wonderful dream.

After lying still for a moment, she heard a rhythmic clicking noise and felt as if someone was staring at her. It was an uncomfortable, penetrating feeling that forced her to open her eyes to see who was disturbing this heavenly moment.

"Ma'am, are you awake?" a girl's British-accented voice asked hesitantly.

Louise made a grunting noise, the sort of noise you make when you're half-awake, but you want to pretend you're still sleeping.

"Thank goodness. Oh, Miss Baxter, I was worried sick," she squeaked.

When Louise heard the name Miss Baxter, she immediately snapped back to her present reality. Now she remembered quite clearly her last lucid moments. On a ship's deck; she was on board some boat…one hundred years ago. *I must still be dreaming*, she thought hazily to herself.

Louise was tucked snugly into a comfortable feather bed, under a pile of royal blue and purple quilts that made it hard for her to sit upright. The four-poster bed she lay in was draped in rich burgundy velvet.

She was not alone in the room. A pretty teenage girl with piercing blue eyes was sitting in a wooden chair at the foot of the bed, knitting. A simple gray dress in an old-fashioned style adorned her slender figure, and a white shawl was tied around her shoulders. Her strawberry blonde hair was pinned back into a tidy bun. Something about her features was weirdly familiar.

"How are you feeling, Miss Baxter? You fainted again on the upper deck. I was terribly worried, ma'am."

Louise couldn't believe that this girl, who looked old enough to be in high school, was calling her ma'am. Actually, it was hard to believe that anyone would call her ma'am; she was only twelve years old.

"I've changed you into your bedclothes. That dress was most constricting; I thought you should be comfortable," the girl explained eagerly.

Louise turned an embarrassed shade of scarlet, as she realized that the soft and silky feeling she'd noticed earlier was from the satin fabric of an unfamiliar slip she was wearing. She pulled the quilt up to try and get a better look at herself. She had never worn a silk nightgown in her life, and the thought of this stranger undressing her and changing her into one was mortifying.

"Do you not like the gown, ma'am? Is everything to your taste? I found it in your steamer trunk. I can put another one on you if you'd prefer."

"No!" Louise answered quickly, alarmed at the sound of her own voice, a bit strange, but very real. "I mean, ummm... no, thank you. That's fine. And, excuse me for asking this, but... who are you?"

"Oh dear, Captain Smith said your memory was a tad foggy. You don't remember me?" the unfamiliar girl asked, her knitting needles paused in mid stitch.

"I'm sorry, but no."

"I am Anna Hard, your maid."

"My *what*?" Louise asked, shocked. *What is happening?*

"Yes, ma'am. Don't worry; the ship's doctor said your memory will gradually return. You just need to get your rest. The doctor will be back to check on you in a bit."

"Anna, where are we?" Louise asked while looking around the elegantly decorated room in awe.

"Why, we're on the White Star Line headed toward New York. Isn't it magnificent?"

"I suppose it is," Louise said as she nodded slowly. And it was. "This is auh-mazing. I just didn't expect to be here. What if my mom starts to worry?"

"Your mother?" Anna repeated, looking confused as she got up from her chair. "Why, she knows you're here, ma'am. She was on the dock at Southampton seeing us off." She placed a cool, wet cloth on Louise's forehead and handed her a crystal glass filled with water. "Please, ma'am, stay in bed. You need some rest."

"Well, maybe a little rest would be okay." Louise sank back into the comfortable downy pillows. Wherever she was, she was definitely getting the first-class treatment. And she certainly didn't mind missing a day of Fairview, where she got anything *but* first-class treatment.

"Please, Miss Baxter, stay put. Mr. Baxter will be here shortly. He'll know what to do."

Louise had forgotten there would soon be a Mr. Baxter to contend with! "Mr. Baxter?" she inquired, shocked. "You mean I have a husband?"

"Goodness no," Anna replied, laughing. "Mr. Baxter is your uncle. He also happens to be your manager, in case you've forgotten that as well. He's booked the adjacent suite, as your mother didn't think it proper for you to travel alone at your age."

"Thank Gawd," Louise said with a sigh of relief. She hadn't

even had a real boyfriend yet. Marriage definitely wasn't on her to-do list. "But why do I have a manager?"

"You're an actress," Anna replied, as though it was the most obvious thing in the world. "How could you possibly manage your career, too? And at only seventeen years old."

"That is unbelievably awesome!" Louise had a sudden gust of energy, realizing she had apparently been granted everything she'd been secretly wishing for. "Anna, I'm glad I'm here. I think this is exactly where I'm supposed to be right now."

Anna shook her head, seemingly amused and a little offset at her, or rather Miss Baxter's, unusual behavior.

She fluffed the pillows under Louise's head and left to prepare some chamomile tea and toast, locking the door behind her.

CHAPTER 13

Once she was alone, Louise pushed off the cumbersome bedding, excited to get up and explore the suite.

The bedroom chamber was paneled with dark cherry wood wainscoting and maroon tapestry wallpaper. There was a decorative fireplace with intricately carved ribbon molding opposite the four-poster bed, and a large still-life oil painting of flowers and fruit hung above the mantel in a gold frame. An opened antique rolltop writing desk in the corner was neatly stacked with White Star Line stationery. Louise tested out a plush chaise lounge that looked like something Scarlett O'Hara would be draped on in *Gone with the Wind*.

The hardwood floor was cold on her bare feet as she tiptoed into a second room off the sleeping cabin. She walked into a parlor furnished with a couch, a loveseat, and two matching armchairs upholstered in an ornate beige-and-gold pattern. The decor was all very formal; nothing looked comfortable or inviting. She thought of a compact little floating palace, elegant, rich, and old-fashioned. Louise noticed there were no windows or portals in this room, either. The wood panels were starting to make her feel like she was in a coffin. She ran her hand along the velvety textured wallpaper as she walked around the circumference of the room.

Louise spotted another, smaller area off the parlor. She padded across an intricate reddish purple Oriental carpet into a separate dressing alcove and closet. A vanity table was covered with bottles of perfume and jars of creams. A powder puff was poofing out of a lilac blue canister of powder, some of which was scattered like snowflakes on the glass. It smelled like a department store at the mall.

A sepia-colored photograph was displayed in between the perfumes. Louise carefully picked up the tarnished frame with the amber-tinted image, so as not to knock over any of the bottles.

She was holding a picture of a beautiful woman wearing a pinkish dress, and clasping a bouquet of pale roses in her hands. Her flawless complexion, dark hair gently falling in waves to her shoulders, and gray eyes framed by long eyelashes made her look like a movie star from Old Hollywood.

"This must be Miss Baxter," Louise whispered to herself, shakily placing the picture frame back on the vanity with trembling fingers.

She walked deeper into the closet, drawn to Miss Baxter's steamer trunk, which was opened in the middle of the room. The black leather trunk had a gold padlock and was more like a wardrobe than any suitcase she had ever seen. It was taller than Louise and deep enough for her to walk right in. This woman did not pack light. It seemed as though someone had been interrupted in the middle of unpacking, as the clothes were in disarray.

Whoever Miss Baxter was, she definitely had an unbelievable closet filled with the most fabulous clothes Louise had ever seen. Dresses of violet chiffon and canary yellow silk with peach ribbons spilled carelessly out onto the floor. A few items had been hung up on hangers in the closet—a fur coat, a dressing gown, and a pink dress that looked exactly like the one Louise had tried on with Brooke at Marla and Glenda's Traveling Fashionista Vintage Sale. It seemed to be the same dress she had been wearing earlier that afternoon on the ship's deck!

Louise once again held the dusky pink dress in her hands. It was unmistakably the same dress she had tried on in the store, except now it was in perfect condition, without a rip or stain anywhere. The downy hairs on her arms stood up as she held the fabric to her nose, inhaled deeply, and found it smelled like perfume and powder, like the way her mother smelled when she was getting dressed to go out to dinner.

Louise closed her eyes to smell the fabric again and was overtaken by a wave of homesickness. She had the same aching feeling once before on the first day of summer camp. She had begged her mom to let her go away to sleepover camp, but then once she got there and was alone on her top bunk, all she wanted to do was be back home again. It seemed to Louise that she was a long way from Timber Trails.

Before she could investigate further, Louise was distracted by a glimmer from the back of the closet. Light was being reflected off what appeared to be a full-length mirror. Slowly, she walked up to the ornately gold-framed mirror on the far side of the closet.

It didn't make any sense. How was she being mistaken for this beautiful, older woman? If this woman was actually Miss Baxter, how could anyone in their right mind mistake Louise for her? Is that who Louise looked like now?

She hesitantly looked up at her reflection and felt a wave of disappointment to see that it was, in fact, herself, twelve-year-old, brace-face, frizzy-haired Louise, staring back from behind the glass. *Really?*

Louise lowered herself carefully to the floor and hugged her knees to her chest. It seemed as though on the inside she was Louise Lambert, but to everyone else she was this Miss Baxter, a gorgeous teenage actress. Definitely rich. Probably even famous. She smiled and unconsciously began twirling a strand of her hair between her thumb and index finger. That was how she did her best thinking, and none of this made any sense. Somehow she had woken up in the body of a woman who was taking a first-class trip on the White Star Line, with her own personal maid and her uncle/manager, from England to New York City. Like, one hundred years ago. She guessed she needed to figure out how to get back to Connecticut and to the twenty-first century... but not quite yet. This was going to be way too much fun to miss.

CHAPTER 14

"Ma chèrie! Have you missed me?" boomed an older singsong male voice from the hallway. *Mr. Baxter?!*

"I've arrived, my precious niece! Have no fear..."

Louise jumped up, ran out of the closet, through the sitting room, slid across the hardwood floor, and dived for the enormous bed. She was still wearing nothing besides the flimsy nightgown Anna had dressed her in, and she certainly did not want to have her first encounter with her manager wearing that. She heard the scratching of a key turning in the lock as she buried herself under the mound of thick aubergine blankets.

The door swung open and in walked Anna carrying a sterling silver tea service. She was followed by a round, squat, middle-aged man wearing pressed khaki pants and a navy blue suit jacket and tie. He had no hair on the top of his head, but overcompensated for it with a bushy handlebar mustache and big caterpillar-like eyebrows.

"I've heard all about your adventures on the high seas. I've come to rescue you!" Mr. Baxter bellowed.

Louise, who was slowly starting to suffocate under all of that down, timidly peeked her eyes and nose out.

"Oh good, Miss Baxter has awoken from her slumber. I've brought Dr. Hastings to check on you."

Anna quickly wrapped Louise up in a buttercup yellow dressing gown made of thick velvet. She was nearly doubled in size covered in all that material. It had a satin sash and a hideous frilly lace collar. Before she could object, Anna plopped a floppy lace hat on her head and tied it under her chin with a yellow ribbon. Louise felt completely ridiculous.

Dr. Hastings, a tall, thin old man, loomed in the doorway, like a vampire waiting to be invited in. He cut a menacing figure with midnight black hair, sunken eyes, and gaunt, hollow cheeks. Wearing a coal black suit and tie, he looked more like a mortician than a doctor. He approached the bedside, and leaned over Louise to feel her forehead with the back of his cold, dry, ghostly pale hand.

"Harrumph," he mumbled by way of introduction, removing a tongue depressor from his black leather medicine bag.

"Say ahhh," he instructed.

Louise hesitantly opened her mouth, and he roughly pressed her tongue down with the flat wooden stick.

"Harrumph, very interesting." Dr. Hastings put the depressor back in his satchel and took out a penlight that he shone directly in her right eye, then her left eye, then her right ear, and finally her left ear, making a "harrumph" noise each time. With surprising force, he pressed his hand on Louise's stomach.

"Ouch!" she cried out, feeling a shooting pain with his touch.

"Well, what is it, Doctor?" Mr. Baxter asked anxiously. "What is all of the harrumphing about?"

Dr. Hastings stood up and looked down at the concerned uncle, who seemed like one of the seven dwarfs next to him.

"Fiber," Dr. Hastings said.

"Excuse me?" asked an incredulous Mr. Baxter.

"She has a severe fiber deficiency. That would explain the tenderness of the stomach and the amnesia."

"Fiber?" Mr. Baxter repeated.

"Yes. She needs to eat five prunes each morning and evening." The doctor began rummaging through his black leather bag. "I'm sure I have some in here."

"Are you a *real* doctor?" Louise asked, rather rudely.

Dr. Hastings looked up angrily. "Of course," he snapped.

As he continued to search his bag for the elusive fibrous fruits, Mr. Baxter stood behind the doctor and started flapping his arms like a bird and puffing air into his cheeks like some bizarre combination of blowfish and chicken. Clearly Mr. Baxter realized what a quack this guy was. Louise was turning bright red as she tried not to laugh, but she couldn't help it. Her eyes were tearing with the effort, and a few giggles escaped her tightly sealed lips.

The doctor emerged triumphantly holding a rusted tin can labeled *Pitted Prunes*. For the first time, there was a flash of life in his murky black eyes.

"This will do the trick!" he exclaimed. "I predict she will have a full recovery in two days' time."

"Pitted prunes! Perfect, my good doctor," Mr. Baxter replied with gusto, patting him heartily on the back and winking at Louise.

Dr. Hastings grumbled one last time in lieu of good-bye and then slunk out of the room.

"Well, at least he didn't try to cure you with leeches," Mr. Baxter joked as he examined the tin of prunes left on the bedside table.

"I guess," Louise responded, not quite getting the humor. That doctor gave her the creeps.

Just then, a handsome man who looked to be in his twenties with slicked-back blond hair and dressed in an old-fashioned charcoal gray three-piece suit poked his head into the room.

"Miss Baxter, my dear. I hear you weren't feeling well this afternoon. I wanted to check in on you."

"Benjamin," Mr. Baxter greeted him curtly, extending his hand to the cute stranger. "She is doing just fine now. Thank you for checking. Although I don't think the timing to be quite appropriate, considering Miss Baxter is trying to get some rest."

"Even when you are under the weather, you still look as beautiful as ever," Benjamin said to Louise with a wink.

Louise blushed. *Did this guy just make up a poem for me?* Unless she was completely off base, totally hot Benjamin was actually flirting with her. And at a time when she must have looked like a two-hundred-pound Little Bo Peep. Didn't Anna realize that no one looks good in this shade of yellow?

"I hope I'll see you both at dinner this evening. Please, Miss Baxter, don't hesitate to call me if you need anything. Anything at all."

"Thank you." Louise nodded and smiled after a long pause, still in shock.

Mr. Baxter hastily showed Benjamin to the door like an overprotective father. He seemed to want to get rid of him as soon as possible. "Guggenheim, what a cad," he muttered as soon as he left the room.

Guggenheim? As in the museum? Louise definitely hoped she would be running into him again soon. Even though that doctor was weird, Benjamin Guggenheim more than made up for it. Finally, she had met someone who was truly crushworthy.

"Perhaps it would do wonders for you to get out of this bed and have a good meal tonight. They say the food on this ship is second to none. We have a fabulous table in the first-class dining salon—Jacob and Madeleine Astor, Isidor Straus—I'm sure his wife, Ida, has been worried sick about you. It would be good if you made an appearance. As they say in the biz, the show must go on!" Mr. Baxter sang as he delicately dabbed his sweaty bald head with a bright pink pocket scarf he had tucked in his jacket pocket.

"Yes, that sounds nice," Louise agreed nonchalantly, trying not to show her enthusiasm, even though she was so excited to get dressed up in Miss Baxter's fabulous dresses and run into Benjamin again.

"Marvelous, I'll leave you to get your beauty sleep. Shall you meet me at the Grand Staircase this evening at half past seven?"

"Sure," Louise mumbled, trying to say as little as possible so he wouldn't catch on that she wasn't the real Miss Baxter. She had no idea how she was going to continue fooling everyone into thinking she was this other woman. How the heck had this happened again?

"Please, my sweet pea, please do try to bring a bit more

energy to the table," Mr. Baxter said, exasperated. "I don't know what's gotten into you. You remind me of a sullen young girl."

Louise raised her eyebrow. He had no clue how right he was.

CHAPTER 15

Mr. Baxter gave a dramatic wave with his flamingo pink handkerchief and left the room. Anna immediately began bustling about, gathering clothes and stockings, and running the bath water. Louise climbed down from the raised bed and stood frozen, not sure what to do with herself.

"Do you need any help?" Louise asked.

Anna stopped dead in her tracks, her arms full of shimmery evening gowns that needed to be hung and pressed.

"Pardon me, ma'am?"

"I said do you need any help? What can I do?"

"Are you still not feeling well, ma'am?" Anna asked, concerned.

"I feel fine. I just feel guilty standing here while you do all the work," Louise replied.

Anna paused and gave her a long, inquisitive look, as

though she were looking at her for the first time. "No, I don't need any help. Why don't you rest? I'm drawing you a bath."

"Can I watch TV?" Louise asked, eyeing the room for a television set or a flat-screen.

"What's Tavee??" Anna repeated, confused.

"Right, never mind," Louise said with a sigh, remembering what era she was in.

She had never rested so much in her life. It was starting to make her anxious. If she was actually lucky enough to be living the life of a fabulous actress, she definitely didn't want to waste it bored and hanging around her room.

"What exactly does Miss Baxter do? I mean, what do I do?" Louise asked, taking off her hideous nightcap.

"What do you do, ma'am? I don't understand." Her maid looked perplexed. Louise wanted to tell her they could be friends. Weren't Anna and Miss Baxter almost the same age anyway?

"Can't we just be friends?" Louise tried hesitantly. Something about the girl's striking blue eyes reminded her of Brooke, and she suddenly wished that she could talk to Anna like she was her friend. It was too painful to think that Brooke wasn't with her on this adventure. They had done pretty much everything together up until this point.

"Ma'am?"

"You don't need to call me that," Louise moaned.

"Sorry, ma'am. I mean, Miss Baxter," Anna stammered, confused.

"Arghh....Not that, either. Never mind. Call me whatever," Louise said, defeated. She dramatically threw herself facedown on the featherbed, clenching her fists in frustration, like a toddler in the midst of a temper tantrum.

"Ahh, that's more like it," she heard Anna whisper to herself. "Ma'am, your bath is drawn."

Louise stepped into the gilded claw-foot bathtub and submerged her head under the warm, soapy water. Ohmigod! Disgusted, she shot out of the water spitting out a salty mouthful of suds. It was *seawater*! Gross.

"Anna, I hate to tell you, but the water in the tap seems to be coming from the ocean," Louise called through the ivory-molded closed door.

"Of course, ma'am!" Anna shouted back. "It's supposed to be therapeutic."

Of course? Louise hastily stepped out of the tub and tried to dry off the sticky residue with the warm, fluffy white bath towel Anna had laid out for her. She guessed there would be a few things that would take some getting used to. Then she had an idea.

"Anna, if you could have one day on this boat to do whatever you wanted, what would it be?" Louise asked, peeking her head out of the bathroom.

"Anything at all?" Anna asked hopefully, fluffing a feather pillow as she expertly made up the bed.

"Anything," Louise confirmed excitedly.

"Well, I suppose I would like to buy a ticket for the swimming pool. Can you believe there's actually a swimming pool on this boat? Wonders never cease."

"Sounds fun," Louise exclaimed, suddenly realizing that Coach Murphy was going to kill her for missing swim practice! She hoped she hadn't missed the Westport meet. She would *never* be able to explain her way out of that one.

"And then I'd like to go relax and take a steam in the Turkish baths. They say it's just like a bath house in Morocco."

"Cool."

"No, they're hot," Anna corrected, still looking a little bewildered that Miss Baxter was offering her all of this.

"Right, that's what I meant. And then?"

"I suppose I'd be hungry, so I'd like to have a meal at the Café Parisien. It's supposed to be just like a real sidewalk café in Paris. Even the waiters are French," she added hesitantly.

"Wow," Louise enthused. "I've always wanted to go to Paris."

"You did a production there last spring," Anna reminded her.

"Of course," Louise responded quickly. "It seems as though my memory is still a bit patchy."

"Perhaps next I would like to ride one of the mechanical

horses in the gymnasium or play cards or take a stroll on the promenade. Not that I've thought this through, of course," she added quickly. Clearly Anna had been thinking this through.

"Sounds perfect," Louise said. "Miss Baxter, I mean, *I* am rich. So let's have fun!"

"You mean we would actually do this? Together?" Anna asked, perplexed.

"Of course," Louise said. "I mean, I've been fainting all day, it really wouldn't be safe for me to spend the day alone."

"Well, in that case..."

"It's settled," Louise said firmly. "Now, Anna, this might seem strange, but with this horrific case of amnesia I seem to have caught, I need a little help in remembering how I talk and act. How does Miss Baxter, I mean, how do *I* behave anyway?"

"I can give you a lesson in becoming Miss Baxter," Anna offered hesitantly.

"Please, maybe that will help spark my memory."

"To begin with, you must flutter your eyelashes a lot. Especially around handsome men," Anna began. "Call everyone 'dahling.' If you like something say, 'It's simply mahvelous.'"

"Mahvelous, dahling," Louise echoed uncertainly.

"Very good," Anna replied. "But you have to add a dramatic flourish to everything you say. Remember, you are an actress."

"Simply mahvelous, dahling," Louise said again, with a little more pizzazz.

"Much better. How do you do?" Anna asked in a posh English accent.

"How do you do?" Louise repeated like an aristocratic parrot.

"Perfect! You should be back to your old self before you know it."

"Now the most important question, what should I wear? Will you help me get ready?" Louise couldn't wait to try on another one of Miss Baxter's fancy dresses.

"I always do," Anna replied, walking into the closet.

"Getting ready" was a process that bore no resemblance to Louise's daily jeans, sneakers, and lip-gloss routine. She gripped the bedpost with white knuckles while Anna strapped her into a corset. She was beginning to feel like an overstuffed Italian sausage. Anna ignored her subject's cries of pain and laced the bustier so tightly Louise thought one of her ribs must have broken.

Glancing down, Louise realized that H&M was knocking off the same look one hundred years later (but a little less painfully)! It was interesting to see how the designs she thought were modern were actually variations on older pieces. On closer examination, she realized the delicate mother-of-pearl buttons and lace trim were unique to this piece and couldn't be mass-produced by any retail chain. She felt a little sad that the intricacies and specialness of the piece had somehow been lost over the years.

Anna helped her into the beautiful violet chiffon tea gown Louise had seen earlier in the steamer trunk. It was accentuated with a spray of hand-sewn grass green and raspberry pink silk flowers that were so delicate they looked like they could only have been stitched by a doll's hands.

"Oh my God, it's a Lucile," Louise whispered loudly while reading the pale green tag with black script lettering. "And it's in perfect condition."

"It better be," Anna replied, smoothing the wrinkles out of the fabric with her hands. "You paid a pretty pound for it last week."

"Oh right, it's new," Louise clarified quickly, realizing that in 1912 this would not be vintage.

"She'll be thrilled to see you wearing it. You look absolutely radiant in her designs."

"When I see her?" Louise asked, confused. "You mean Lucile is on this ship, too?"

"Yes, don't you remember? Lady Duff-Gordon and Sir Cosmo are both on board. They are traveling to New York to open her first American Lucile shop," Anna answered patiently, as though she was speaking to a slow five-year-old.

To her surprise, the dress fit Louise perfectly. It was like it

was custom-made especially for her. "That is so cool," she breathed, excited.

"Would you like me to warm the dress up for you?" Anna asked as she extended her arm, confused.

"No, I just meant this is really nice. This will be classic." Louise carefully chose her words. "We should take care of this one." She ran her hands reverently over the delicate, sheer fabric. She had just seen a mesmerizing retrospective exhibit of Lucile designs at the Met Costume Institute in New York City. Each dress was so uniquely and beautifully crafted and painstakingly sewn, Louise thought she could still feel the love and emotion that went into each piece, even after all of those years.

"Yes, ma'am." Anna nodded, giving Louise a curious look and handing her a matching purple silk shawl. "You should take a wrap as well; the air is quite brisk."

Louise was spritzed with some musky French perfume, powdered, and adjusted and, eventually, she was ready to go. She didn't have to lift a finger; it was like being sent through a car wash.

CHAPTER 16

Anna and Louise stepped out into the carpeted hallway. It looked like they were staying in a fancy hotel. The ivory-colored inlaid walls were lined with shiny brass light fixtures and sconces.

"Should we buy a ticket for the swimming pool?" Anna asked excitedly.

After experiencing exactly how unbelievably long it took for Miss Baxter to get dressed, Louise wasn't quite as psyched about jumping into a pool. For the first time in her life, she had turned into one of those girls who didn't want to get her hair wet.

"How about a stroll on the upper deck instead?" Anna suggested quickly, sensing Louise's lack of enthusiasm.

"Perfect," Louise piped up, relieved.

Anna led her down the hall to an old-fashioned elevator

that was operated by a mustached man in a White Star uniform. "Where to, ladies?" he asked jovially.

"The upper deck, please," Louise replied confidently, feeling fancy and sophisticated in her new dress.

They had elevators one hundred years ago? This boat was more amazing than any modern cruise ship she had ever known! He closed the wrought-iron gate and manually started the lift. "Going up."

At this time of day, the ship's decks were crowded with passengers taking leisurely walks and enjoying the sunlight. Children in woolen knickers and newsboy caps were running races up and down the deck and spinning tops on the wooden floorboards. Uniformed men were walking French poodles on long leashes. Women were strolling in small groups laughing and gossiping. She could get used to a life of leisure!

Looking around, Louise noticed that everyone seemed to be wearing hats. Men wore bowler hats or fancier silk top hats. Women wore much more elaborate hats with wide brims and long narrow plumes sticking out of them. Louise thought they looked really cool and decided she was going to try and bring back the fashion when she returned to school.

They passed a group of children laughing and playing a ring toss game.

"It must be past noon," Anna said as she squinted up at the direct angle the sun was shining down on them. Glancing down at her bare wrist, Louise realized she never wore a watch because she always relied on her cell phone for the time. She was pretty clueless without it. Since her parents were so concerned about radiation, that was about all her phone was good for: a clock. She wondered where her cell was now—still in the pocket of her jean jacket on the hardwood floor of the vintage sale?

"Miss Baxter, I don't see any other maids on the A Deck. People may think it's a little odd for us to be walking together like this."

"Really?" Louise asked, surprised that anyone would care. It seemed weird, since it felt like she was just hanging out with her friend.

"Miss Baxter! How lovely to see you out and about on this fine day," an unfamiliar female voice called to her.

Louise slowly raised her head. She had forgotten that people who she had never seen in her life would recognize her and think she knew them. A young woman, wearing a sea foam green dress that flowed gracefully over her very pregnant belly and accessorized with a blinding amount of diamonds and sapphires, was waving at them. She was beautiful, with hazel eyes and a perfectly dainty nose and cherub pout. She couldn't have been more than eighteen years old.

"Who is that woman?" Louise asked Anna under her breath.

"Madeleine Astor," Anna whispered.

"Mrs. Astor," Louise said in her most grown-up voice. "How do you do?"

"Just fine, thank you. This sea air does wonders for the spirit, don't you find?" Mrs. Astor replied, without showing any inclination that she was having a conversation with a twelve-year-old girl. Her green-and-purple-feathered hat made her look like a proud peacock.

"Yes, it's simply mahvelous," Louise sang in a saccharine-sweet tone, trying to remember Anna's lesson. She felt as though they were both actors in a play for which she didn't know the lines. She had a feeling that if she didn't end this conversation soon, she would be discovered as a phony. Her heart started racing.

"I'm sorry we can't chat, but Anna and I must run," Louise said. "We have an appointment with a mechanical horse, I believe."

Anna giggled, and Louise bit her bottom lip so she wouldn't laugh.

"Oh, I see. Do you have a session with that darling English chap, Mr. McCawley?" Mrs. Astor asked, eyeing Louise's, or rather Miss Baxter's, slim figure. "Although I don't see why you need to be exercising at all. You'll simply disappear. I see you are bringing your help with you?"

"I find exercising to be such a bore." Louise forced a dra-

matic yawn. "But *my friend* Anna and I do love a good horse-back ride, don't you, Mrs. Astor?"

"I suppose," she replied, giving them both a strange look.

"Ta-ta for now," Louise called over her shoulder as she and Anna hastily continued down the deck, hardly able to suppress their giggles. But before they had walked more than a few feet, Louise doubled over in pain, clutching her stomach. She suddenly felt as if someone were wringing out her intestines like a wet towel.

"I'm going to be sick," she moaned and ran over to the side of the boat. Then she promptly threw up. Anna held her hair back from her face and shielded her from the curious yet averted glances of the other passengers.

Sweating and weak, Louise lowered herself gingerly to the deck floor. She started crying; she couldn't help it. Ever since she was a little girl, she cried every time she got sick. Suddenly she felt like she was five years old again. She wanted her mother.

Anna sat herself down on the floor next to Louise. "The first time I was on a boat I got really seasick, too. It's just awful."

"Yes," Louise agreed. "That must be it. Seasickness..." But for some reason, she wasn't completely convinced. Echoes of the stabbing pain she had felt in her stomach seconds ago lingered on. It reminded her of the time she had gotten food poisoning on vacation with Brooke's family. At that moment, Louise wished that she were back in her own house curled up on the couch watching an old black-and-white movie.

Anna took a neatly folded handkerchief out of her pocket and handed it to Louise so she could wipe her mouth. "At least it's not windy," she added with a chuckle. Despite her miserable state, Louise laughed, imagining what a mess she would be in right now if the wind had not been blowing in her favor.

They looked at each other and started laughing.

The clacking of shoes against the hard wooden planks gave the girls a start. They stifled their giggles and looked up as two passengers strolled by, arms linked, out for a romantic stroll. A fair-haired lady carrying a parasol glanced down as she passed, giving Louise and Anna a confused and snooty look.

The girls got up, and Anna led them toward the gymnasium. A little seasickness was not going to stop Louise from enjoying her fabulous day as this old-fashioned, glamorous actress.

CHAPTER 17

"Wow, what a cool room," Louise said while checking out the old-fashioned exercise bikes, rowing machines, and two strange contraptions that looked a lot like a camel and a horse. The floor was tiled white with black diamonds, and the oak wood paneling seemed more suited for a library than a gym. A brown leather punching bag was suspended from one of the exposed wooden ceiling beams in the center of the room.

"What on earth is this for?" Louise asked, pointing to the camel-like machine, perplexed.

"Exercise, of course." Anna gave Louise a look like she was from Mars.

"Weird," Louise remarked, realizing that Anna would probably have the same reaction if she came to the Fairview Sports Club and saw an elliptical trainer or a Pilates machine for the first time.

"Good morning, ladies," a thick Cockney accent called out from behind one of the camels.

The girls jumped, startled, having thought they were alone.

A sturdy, muscular little man emerged from behind the mechanical camel's hind legs and walked over to Louise and Anna with an outstretched hand.

He was wearing a white polo shirt, white cotton shorts, and white sneakers, which offset his deep tan complexion. He had a toothbrush mustache like Charlie Chaplin, Louise's favorite comic actor from the silent film era.

"I'm T. W. McCawley," he said while shaking both of their hands vigorously.

"I'm Lou...I mean, I'm Miss Baxter." Louise quickly corrected herself mid sentence. "And this is Anna, my friend." Anna smiled at her new title.

"Jolly-o. Are you ready for some exercise? It's been a slow morning; lazy chaps on this ship," T. W. said, gesturing to the empty gymnasium. "Excuse my frankness, but it's a shame to see this modern equipment sit idle."

Louise and Anna nodded mutely in agreement.

"Well, you aren't exactly dressed for exercise," he observed, looking them over in their long dresses. "But I have yet to meet a dame who was. I suppose the rowing machine is out. And the swimming pool."

"Oh, I'm on the swim team!" Louise blurted out. T. W. and

Anna both looked at her, confused, and then T. W. started chuckling.

"Right, right, and I'm on the Olympic equestrian team," he replied sarcastically.

Louise felt her face burn hot with indignation. She wasn't lying. If Brooke were here, she would vouch for her. But then she realized that in this era maybe girls didn't play team sports like they did one hundred years later.

"Perhaps I can interest you ladies in a camel ride? It's like being in the Moroccan desert; you simply need to use a little imagination." Louise could not believe this was the treadmill of the early twentieth century. And that she was about to exercise in a genuine Lucile dress.

"Yes, please," Anna replied gleefully, hopping on the mechanical horse as though she had been doing it all her life.

Louise clumsily climbed on top of the other machine, getting the hem of her purple chiffon gown caught in the stirrups.

"That's the ticket!" T. W. shouted. "I like a dame with a little spunk." He turned on the machines, and the animals jerked into motion.

Louise burst out laughing. Some man just called her a dame, and how exactly was this toning her problem areas? Brooke would have died if she could see her like this. She was having too much fun to go home yet, but she also didn't entirely want to have any more experiences without her best friend.

The machines ground to an abrupt halt, and T. W. suddenly grabbed Louise around the waist and hoisted her off the camel. Louise watched Anna dismount like a gymnast.

"Don't want to overexert yourself," he said protectively.

Overexert? He had clearly never been to one of Mr. Murphy's Saturday morning swim practices.

"See you ladies again tomorrow!" T. W. exclaimed in his upbeat tone. After several more bone-crushing handshakes, Anna and Louise left the gymnasium and stepped back out into the main corridor. So far it seemed playing the part of Miss Baxter was going to be a lot easier and more fun than she had thought!

CHAPTER 18

"I think we go this way to the café." Anna pushed open a set of double doors. "Oops, wrong entrance," she said sheepishly.

They had accidentally walked into the ship's library. The room was paneled with floor-to-ceiling bookshelves, all filled with hundreds of leather-bound volumes. There was a dark wooden ladder propped up against one wall to help reach the upper shelves.

A few bespectacled men were sitting in forest green club chairs at dark mahogany tables flipping through newspapers or books. One man glanced up and raised his eyebrows, apparently surprised to see two women in a room otherwise occupied by men.

Louise loved libraries. When she was a little kid, she had made it a goal to read every book in the children's section. Somehow, when she was five, and could barely read by herself, that seemed feasible. But now that she was twelve, and read all the time, she realized how unrealistic that idea was. It was kind of sad and overwhelming now when she thought about it.

She walked over to one of the walls and picked out a dark red bound novel at random.

"This is one of my mom's favorite movies. Judy Garland is incredible...." Louise said, trailing off. Most likely *The Wizard of Oz* hadn't been made into a film yet, so she probably shouldn't say any more. "Anna, shouldn't you be in school now?" Louise added, thinking once again that she would be in big trouble if she didn't show up for classes.

"In school? At my age?" Anna said with a shrug. "You really must have hit your head. I finished last year, and I've been working for you since then. But soon I'd like to get married and start my own family."

"How old are you?" Louise tried to keep her jaw from dropping. Maybe Anna was one of those people who looked really, really good for, what was she, thirty?

"Seventeen. But not for long; I'll be eighteen next month. In a few years, I'll be an old maid!" Anna said. Louise laughed, but Anna didn't crack a smile.

"Do you have a boyfriend?" Louise did her best to play along.

"Well, there's someone, I suppose." Anna blushed and lowered her gaze. "He works on this ship. We have been spending a bit of time together. He's so handsome."

"That's great. I'd love to meet him!" Louise exclaimed, happy for her new friend. Who was this guy?

"Pssst," a voice hissed from behind a paper. "Pssst."

Louise's eyes darted over to Anna. Were they being too loud?

"Psssst." The sound was coming from behind a newspaper at a nearby table.

The *Atlantic Daily Bulletin* lowered, revealing Benjamin Guggenheim's face.

"I was hoping I would run into you. But I see you've found me out instead."

Louise blushed. "I didn't mean to, I mean, we were just passing through."

"Well, I am certainly glad you did. Can you believe this ship has its own daily paper?" he asked as he folded up his periodical and got to his feet, linking his arm through Louise's elbow. With his chiseled jaw line and intense green eyes, he was even more handsome than Louise remembered. "Let's go for a walk, shall we?"

CHAPTER 19

"It's a bit brisk. Perhaps you can get Miss Baxter a coat?"

"Yes, sir," Anna replied to Mr. Guggenheim, rushing off before Louise had a chance to argue. They were walking outside on the partly shaded first-class promenade.

"Well, Miss Baxter, I must say, I've been hoping we would have a chance to take a stroll," he said as they walked slowly along the ship's wooden deck.

Why couldn't Todd act a little bit more like this? Louise wondered, thinking back to the embarrassing scene that played out in the school hallway yesterday. *Where did all the chivalrous men go?*

Louise looked down, blushing. She was burning up, despite the freezing temperature. Brisk wasn't the word for it—they seemed to be taking the arctic route to New York.

"Isn't the view marvelous?" he asked her, arms clasped behind his back.

"Yes," Louise replied. "I love the ocean." The sky was a clear and cloudless expanse reflecting off the never-ending calm cerulean blue sea.

They walked quietly, turning around at the bow to retrace the same steps. The boat must have been a mile long.

"And the ship is truly the epitome of opulence, is it not?"

"Yes, it is," Louise replied enthusiastically, secretly realizing she was starting to get bored. *Do these people actually speak about anything?* She had never exchanged so many pleasantries in her life.

"I love your museum," she began, trying to steer the conversation toward something more interesting, like art. And it was truly one of her favorites.

Her parents had taken her into New York City to see a Julian Schnabel retrospective at the Guggenheim Museum last summer. She remembered how magical it had felt the first time she had walked up the magnificent white spiral walkway under the skylight while looking at some of the most beautiful modern abstract paintings she had ever seen. Some were made on broken plates, some on green army tarps, some on velvet. She saw a whole landscape within those brushstrokes. She could have stayed in that rotunda forever.

"My museum?" Benjamin replied, seemingly perplexed. "What exactly are you referring to, my dear?"

Oops. Does the Guggenheim Museum not exist yet?

Louise panicked. "I'm sorry, I mean, your...castle." He gave her a confused look.

"I mean your...your estate," Louise stammered. *This guy must have an estate, right?* "It's so beautiful it reminds me of a museum."

He was still looking at her strangely. "Thank you. Please come back for a visit whenever it suits. We would love to have you."

We?

They continued walking, but she had no idea what to say next. Was he referring to his girlfriend? His wife? His mom? She was pretty sure he was flirting with her, so maybe he still lived with his parents? Louise was cold and exhausted. She wished she could just be herself.

"Can we sit, please?" she asked as they passed one of the many ornate iron and wooden benches situated throughout the deck.

"That sounds like a marvelous idea," Benjamin replied, helping her to the seat.

They sat in an awkward silence. Pretending to be this other girl was totally tiring and not really as much fun as she thought it would be.

Louise snapped out of her reverie and turned to see Anna stumbling toward her, arms full of velvet and fur and feathers, her eyes barely visible through the plumes.

"Anna!" she called, excited and relieved to see a friendly face. Laughing, Louise rushed over to help her friend. She plucked the ostrich-feathered hat off the top of the pile and helplessly tried to arrange it on her own head.

"You are an odd one, Miss Baxter," Mr. Guggenheim said. "Shall I escort you ladies to the Verandah Café for afternoon tea? It's about time for me to enjoy a cigar in the smoking room before supper."

"Yes, please," Louise answered quickly.

Anna helped Louise into a burgundy velvet coat that cinched her waist with a nauseatingly tight belt. The cuffs were decorated with huge puffs of fur; it was like she had two chinchillas wrapped around her wrists. The coat barely skimmed the floor, making it difficult to walk without a serious risk of falling flat on her face.

"Splendid," Anna remarked while carefully rearranging Louise's hat and hair. The coat seemed to weigh about fifty pounds, and Louise was already sweating underneath the weight of all of that fabric. She thought she must have looked utterly ridiculous.

Benjamin led them through a smoke-filled, mahogany-paneled clubroom that smelled strongly of cigars and cedar that adjoined the Verandah Café. "Well, I will leave you two ladies for now." He removed his gray bowler hat with a flourish and bowed down to kiss Louise's hand, back to being his

dashing self. "Miss Baxter, I look forward to seeing you again this evening for dinner."

"Thank you, Mr. Guggenheim," Louise said with a smile.

And with that, he spun around and left. It was a completely opposite feeling than she'd had when he'd first come to the room this morning, but thank Gawd.

CHAPTER 20

Anna and Louise walked through a glass-paneled set of fancy oak-lined doors. The café was bright and airy, with natural sunlight streaming throughout the room. The walls were crawling with trellises covered with bright green ivy right down to the black-and-white checkerboard tile floor. The room was filled with elegantly dressed ladies chatting and daintily sipping from china teacups.

"There's Lady Duff-Gordon," Anna whispered to Louise, pointing to a woman seated alone on the far side of the café. She was sitting in a white wicker chair at a corner table by a grand arched window with an amazing view of the ocean, and she gave them an enthusiastic wave. Louise froze. She could not believe that she was actually seeing the designer of Lucile, a legend, alive and in person.

"You should take tea with her. I best be heading back to the suite to take care of the rest of the unpacking before dinner," Anna said and then gave Louise's hand an encouraging squeeze. Once again, she left the room before Louise could protest.

Lady Lucy Duff-Gordon was probably not the most beautiful woman Louise had ever seen, but she was definitely one of the most stylish. She wore a pastel green lace dress, the color of a dew-stained grassy meadow on a spring morning, which was tied at the waist with an ivory silk sash. Lucile's trademark silk flowers were pinned to her breast. She wore an elegant strand of pearls looped three times around her neck and a simple matching green broad-rimmed hat.

"Hello, Lucile, it's such a pleasure to see you again," Louise blurted out, unable to mask the excitement in her voice.

If she could have picked ten historic figures to have tea with, Lucile would definitely have made the list. She was one of the most famous British fashion designers from the early twentieth century and one of Louise's personal favorites, right behind Coco Chanel, Karl Lagerfeld, and Vivienne Westwood. She was one of the first fashion designers to create more feminine and practical clothes for women—with revealing necklines and long slit skirts that you could actually walk in, not to mention a very popular line of lingerie. She dressed all of the chicest royalty and stars of her time. There was a whole chapter dedicated to her in Louise's vintage book.

"Please, darling, all of my intimate friends call me Lucy,"

she said, rising to give Louise an air kiss on both cheeks. "Tea?" Lucy asked Louise and signaled to a waiter carrying a tray of scones and cream.

"Please," Louise said with a nod. "That sounds lovely." And it really did.

"Isn't this ship divine?" Lucile asked and took a delicate sip of tea from a fancy bone china cup. "I just love my pretty little cabin with its electric heater and pink curtains."

"It's magical," Louise agreed, in more ways than one. She tried to sit very still and straight in her rickety white wicker chair so the towering blue-green ostrich plume protruding from her hat wouldn't be waving around like a flag in the wind. She was having minimal success in that endeavor.

"How did you start designing?" Louise asked as a waiter carrying a polished silver platter delivered her a fresh pot of tea. She didn't want to seem like a reporter for her school newspaper, the *Fairview Press,* but she couldn't help herself. She wasn't going to pass up this opportunity to interview one of her idols in person.

"Well, I suppose it was out of necessity. After my first husband and I divorced, I was left absolutely penniless. It was then I realized I would have to rely on my own wits and talent to put food on the table. So I set up a dressmaking business, which had always been a passion of mine. It's nice to have a man around, but darling, you can't count on them."

"Yes, I definitely agree with you." Louise was happy to discover that Lucy was totally turning out to be a cool, modern woman. "But how do you create your designs?" Louise pressed on, taking a sip of English breakfast tea and choosing a black currant scone, which she greedily slathered with raspberry jam, happy to discover that food in 1912 seemed pretty delicious so far.

"The creative process is a magical thing," Lady Lucy replied, carefully setting down her teacup in its saucer. She had a strong nose and sharp cheekbones, giving off a distinguished and aristocratic air. "But there is a reason why my dresses are known as *emotional gowns*. I like to truly know my clients, and I believe their dresses should be a material representation of their personality. The cut, the color, the style, all of these elements should be a reflection of that particular woman. I see myself as a psychologist as much as a dressmaker."

"That's amazing," Louise said in awe, wiping a glob of jam from her upper lip. "I see you as an artist."

"Thank you. I don't want to dress only the body of the woman; I want to dress her soul," Lady Lucy continued with a flourish. "What I am searching for in my designs is both truth and beauty. Just because you may be the same size as another woman, doesn't mean you should be wearing the same gown."

"How wonderful," Louise said with a sigh. "The dresses are, like, personalized."

"Of course, my dear. I spent months sewing your pink gown by hand. And I do feel I succeeded in capturing your alluring spirit. You look absolutely beguiling in it." Lady Duff-Gordon looked out at the sea through the arched window, lost in thought. "Perhaps that dress will always carry a little bit of both of our spirits in it. That's one way to cheat death, now, isn't it? Sorry to be so morose on such a glorious afternoon."

"That's fine," Louise said. "I'm generally pretty morose." Going to Fairview Junior High could put any halfway sane person in a bad mood.

"I have an unusual idea I want to run by you." Lucile turned to her, rather, to Miss Baxter. "I had a dream the other night that there was a parade of walking mannequins, all wearing my dresses. Isn't that surreal?"

"Like a catwalk?" Louise asked and then took another bite of the yummy scone. "In a fashion show?"

"Not cats, dear, *women*," Lucy clarified, not understanding Louise's modern term. "But, yes, it would be a show of fashion. It would be as entertaining to watch as a play. I would have glorious, goddess-like girls, who would walk to and fro dressed in my models, displaying them to the best advantage to an admiring audience of women. Exactly!" she trilled, clapping her hands.

"Good idea." Louise grinned knowingly. "I think that will be a big success."

"I just met these two peculiar ladies who seemed to know precisely what I was talking about. They want to help style the first show. What were their names? Glenda? Marla? Never mind..."

"You know Marla and Glenda?" Louise asked excitedly. Maybe they were the same women who gave her the dress at the Traveling Fashionista Vintage Sale. Maybe they could explain exactly how Louise ended up here. "One woman is tall with red hair, the other shorter and plainer. Both kind of witchy..."

"Why, yes, I believe those were the two women who were talking to me about the parade of walking girls over a card game this afternoon. Very eccentric ladies?"

"Yes." Louise nodded quickly. "Do you know where they may be? It's very urgent I find them."

"No, dear, they said they would find me when I needed them. Very peculiar."

"Well, please let them know I am looking for them if they turn up. And thank you," Louise added, not able to suppress a twinge of sadness at the culture she grew up in. She couldn't believe how much time and thought went into clothes at one time. She hoped that fashion was not a dying art.

"I suppose I should be going," Louise decided, swallowing

a last gulp of lukewarm tea. She felt bad leaving Anna for so long, even though she was having such a great time. "Anna is expecting me."

"You've got me thinking a bit," Lady Duff-Gordon said, distracted. "I think I'll stay for another cup of tea before dinner."

Louise stood up slowly, so as not to disrupt the precarious feathered installation towering over her, and excused herself from the table. She walked quickly through the café and out on the deck before realizing that she would have to rely on the kindness of strangers (or rather one particularly cute porter) to show her back to her stateroom.

CHAPTER 21

Anna was waiting for her in the suite with Miss Baxter's evening outfit laid out on the bed. She had selected a twilight blue evening gown with a plunging neckline and lace cap sleeves. Louise picked up the dress reverently, admiring the intricate beadwork on the bodice.

"It's perfect!" Louise squealed with delight, throwing off her heavy velvet cloak and hat.

However, Louise was not looking forward to being strapped back into that gut-wrenching corset. Not like she had a choice in the matter. Anna laced her up even more tightly than the last time. It felt like her internal organs were being squashed and rearranged inside her. How exactly did women wear these on a daily basis?

Anna slid the elaborately layered gown over Louise's head. The silky fabric swooshed down over her corseted body, and the tiny navy blue beads made a faint tinkling noise as they

fell down around her. The gown stopped right above the floor, with a little beaded train trailing behind her.

"Oh my," Anna said with a sigh, shaking her head with disappointment. "You seem to have gotten a bit of sun today."

Like that's a bad thing? Louise wondered, happy to have a slight tan in April.

Anna covered Louise's face and lips with a thick white pancakey foundation that came from a brass tin. Louise glanced in the antique mirror behind Anna's shoulder and was once again startled to see herself, now pale as a ghost. She really hoped Anna wouldn't turn around and see the real Louise under all that makeup. Anna used a dark kohl pencil to line her eyes and a brush to smudge it around. She then applied a creamy rouge to her cheeks, making them pop like candy apples. *Apparently, in 1912, the clown look is in style?*

She blotted Louise's lips with a creamy red lipstick. The color was amazing, like Old Hollywood in a golden tube. She sprayed her with a different perfume; this one was a little more floral than the last. Not only could Miss Baxter not wear the same thing twice, it seemed she also couldn't smell like the same thing twice.

Anna placed a delicate diamond tiara on top of her hair, which she had artfully twisted into a loose knot at the nape of her neck with a few strategically placed hairpins. Now she was truly a princess, or rather a glamorous actress, with the crown and all.

Looking her over approvingly, Anna handed her a delicate gold mesh clutch to hold her lipstick and perfectly accessorize the look. *Voilà.*

Of course, Louise had no idea how to find the first-class dining room by herself. Anna insisted on drawing her a map on a piece of White Line stationery from the writing desk so that she wouldn't be late for dinner. Louise took the map and left the suite, slowly making her way through the grandiose corridors, teetering on Miss Baxter's pinching blue satin high-heeled shoes. The carpeted hallways all looked the same, and she was relieved to have some direction.

She nodded mutely in greeting to the other passengers she passed. The corset made it hard for her to breathe, let alone talk. It was strange; they all looked like they were cast as extras in a period film. Men were handsomely dressed in dark dinner jackets with top hats. Women had their hair in elaborate up-dos, and some wore floor-length skirts that looked like brightly colored lampshades and were gathered so tightly at the ankle they were forced to waddle down the hall like a flock of ducks. To her, it was a very peculiar style.

"Isn't it simply divine?" she overheard one woman gush. "Have you ever seen a ship so luxurious?" Everyone seemed to be in the best of spirits.

After two lefts and a right, Louise arrived.

CHAPTER 22

Standing at the top of the grandest staircase she had ever seen, Louise basked in the natural moonlight that shone through the wrought-iron-and-glass dome above her head. She looked up in awe and saw a black night sky flecked with twinkling stars, flashing down on her like a celestial paparazzi. The staircase was constructed of polished oak and embellished with gilded bronze decorations. Ornately framed oil landscape paintings decorated the walls of the landing. A bronze cherub mounted on the center railing held up a lamp that illuminated the way. Walking down the wide sweeping stairs in Miss Baxter's evening gown made her feel truly beautiful and special, like maybe she could actually be Miss Baxter for real.

"Ahh, Miss Baxter!" Mr. Baxter shouted from the foot of the staircase. "Aren't you a sight for sore eyes?"

Louise blushed as all eyes looked up at her. She heard a low whistle from a man in a black tailcoat passing by her on the stairs. *Awesome, I'm a movie star!* She wasn't used to being noticed by men—or rather boys—for her beauty. She carefully made her way down the staircase, convinced she was going to wipe out in Miss Baxter's unfamiliar high-heeled shoes and be totally humiliated. With a little patience, and some help from the smooth wooden handrail, she made it safely down to the ground level.

Louise looked down at her hand on the banister and gasped. She was wearing a stunning diamond-and-sapphire ring on her right ring finger. She held the ring up to the natural light in awe of the stone's glimmering beauty. Had she been wearing it all along? For some reason, she was a little freaked out that she hadn't noticed it before, and now that she did, her hand felt heavy and weighted down. The ring was spectacular, but it wasn't hers. She had the sudden realization that this wasn't her life. But she quickly pushed those thoughts aside and instead took Mr. Baxter's outstretched hand. He was all gussied up for dinner, wearing a formal tux with a white bow tie and black-and-white wing tip shoes. It looked as though he had greased his handlebar mustache for the occasion, which now turned up in two perfect points.

"Is something wrong with your hip?" he asked, concerned as she held on to his arm for support and hobbled into the dining room through two open French double doors.

"Oh no, my hip is fine," Louise said quickly, embarrassed. "I'm just not used to these shoes or something."

How long would she be able to get away with pretending to be Miss Baxter before she was exposed for who she really was?

CHAPTER 23

The first-class dining room was crowded with hundreds of passengers, all dressed in their evening best. Dinner was clearly the most important social event of the day on this cruise. The ladies were wearing a rainbow of evening gowns, and the men were dressed in tuxedos or formal dark suits with vests, the kind they would put pocket watches into. The room sparkled as the elaborate crystal chandelier in the center of the ceiling cast a soft light that reflected off the women's jewelry. Louise had never seen so many diamonds in her life. The enormous cream-colored room, which seemed to span the width of the entire ship, was strangely familiar. She felt like she had been there before.

Mr. Baxter led her past the other tables, all covered in crisp, white linen tablecloths and set with fine white china with cobalt blue and gold borders. Big porcelain vases filled with beautiful yellow daffodils served as the centerpieces of the tables, as fresh as if they had just been picked. A string orchestra of violins and cellos playing in the corner serenaded the guests. The musicians were dressed in matching white dinner jackets and bow ties.

"Lucy! Cosmo!" Mr. Baxter called across the dining room as he navigated his way through the crowd.

"So nice to see you again, my dear," Lucile exclaimed. "And Henry, you are looking quite well."

There was a flourish of air kisses as Lucy and Cosmo stood up to greet them. Lucy was wearing a white silk evening gown of her own design, embroidered with gold and jeweled dragons. It was spectacular. Her chestnut brown hair was pulled back in an intricate knot, held in place by a jeweled comb, with some curls framing her face.

"Fancy strawberries in April, and in mid ocean. The whole thing is positively uncanny. Why, you would think you were at the Ritz," she remarked.

That would explain Louise's feeling of déjà vu. She had stayed at the Ritz Carlton once with her mom in London, and this dining room was very similar to the restaurant in the hotel.

"I went to the Ritz once with my mother," Louise said to no one in particular, wishing that her mom could see this place, too. Somehow it seemed less special if she couldn't share it with her. Like, how would she know if it had really happened?

"Miss Baxter, that dress looks stunning on you. I need to use you as one of my models," Lucile enthused, turning toward her.

Louise smiled shyly. *The* Lucile was actually asking her—well, Miss Baxter, but still—to be one of her models. It was too surreal. "I love this dress. I'm such a fan of your designs," she gushed, brushing her fingers over the beads.

"Aren't you a dear? You will have to pass by my new salon in New York. We'll fit you for some new dresses."

"Really?" Louise asked excitedly. "Awesome."

Lucy cocked her plucked left eyebrow. "Is that a new term? I am so out of touch these days. I hardly get out of the atelier."

"I suppose so." Louise shut her mouth quickly, realizing her mistake; she'd have to be a little more careful with what slang she used.

"Yes, I would be thrilled to create some more splendid dresses especially for you," Lucile declared.

"Thank you," Louise called over her shoulder as Mr. Baxter continued leading her through the crowded dining room toward their table. Louise thought she might be the luckiest girl in the world at this moment. She just wished she had someone to share it with.

CHAPTER 24

"Mrs. Astor!" Mr. Baxter shouted to the woman Louise had met earlier on the deck, who was now wearing a floor-length salmon-colored evening dress with lace sleeves and waving enthusiastically from a few tables down. He grabbed Louise's hand and hurried her over to their assigned dinner table.

Louise spotted the captain's table at the far side of the room. Captain Smith was seated at a round table with a woman who seemed to be his wife, the first officer, and some other uniformed men whom she didn't recognize.

She caught a glimpse of Dr. Hastings sitting at a nearby table with two female companions in broad-rimmed hats that shadowed their faces. He scowled at Louise and Mr. Baxter as they rushed by, visibly displeased to see his patient ignoring his strict orders. The fine hairs on the back of Louise's neck prickled; that man gave her the creeps.

"Don't you look marvelous," Mr. Baxter gushed to Madeleine Astor, kissing her on both cheeks.

"Oh, Henry, you are too kind. I'm as big as this ship," Mrs. Astor replied, patting her pregnant belly, eyes sparkling. "Miss Baxter, we're so pleased you'll be joining us," she said, turning to Louise. "We were worried you wouldn't feel up to it."

Louise smiled mutely. She still had no idea what to say to this woman.

"Yes, she's feeling a bit under the weather, aren't you?" Mr. Baxter responded, giving her hand a painful squeeze.

"Yes," Louise whispered. Mr. Baxter pulled out a dining chair for her, and she took her place at the table in between Mr. Baxter and Mrs. Astor.

"Mrs. Straus! Jacob! Benjamin! Isidor! Wonderful to see you all on such a fine night as we have here," Mr. Baxter exclaimed enthusiastically.

Louise turned bright red as Benjamin Guggenheim gave her a suave, conspiratorial smile from across the table. She had been looking forward to seeing him since this afternoon, and now she couldn't think of a single thing to say. She gave a quiet "hello" and then shyly glanced down at all of the forks and knives lined up next to the china plate. For the first time in her life, she was grateful that her mother had insisted on their formal dinners in the dining room.

"Champagne, madam?" asked a waiter in a white jacket, popping open a bottle.

"No, thank you," Louise demurred.

"She's only seventeen," Mr. Baxter's voice boomed, waving away the champagne bottle.

"Caviar?" another uniformed waiter asked, holding a silver service tray piled high with a mound of black glistening fish eggs.

"No, thank you," Louise repeated.

"She's been ill," Mr. Baxter offered, throwing up his hands in a gesture of defeat. He turned to Louise with a puzzled expression. "But you love caviar," he remarked in a baffled voice. "What's gotten into you?"

"Not anymore," Louise replied.

He stared into her eyes for a moment, not quite able to place his finger on exactly what was different, and then hastily drank his champagne in one gulp.

"Miss Baxter, isn't this ship fabulous? Bruce Ismay has really outdone himself this time. Have you ever seen such luxury?" asked a sturdy woman sitting opposite Louise. Mr. Baxter had referred to her earlier as Ida Straus.

"No, Mrs. Straus, I haven't," Louise agreed. And she really hadn't.

"We were just speaking about one of your productions," Mrs. Astor said, turning to Louise, as the men talked about business among themselves. "Simply brilliant. You are a true talent, my dear."

"Thank you." Louise felt strangely proud that she was apparently a famous actress. She was starting to take all these compliments personally.

"Do you have anything in the works?" Mrs. Straus asked in a conspiratorial tone, hoping to get some juicy gossip.

"I don't know," Louise answered honestly, picking up a glass of lemon water.

"Well, it's a tough business, but you have a good manager. It's nice to keep it in the family," Mrs. Astor interjected, nodding to Mr. Baxter.

Mrs. Straus smiled warmly and raised her glass to Louise. "Cheers to that, darling."

Louise let out a yelp of surprise as she suddenly felt a socked foot suggestively touch her ankle. Was someone actually trying to play footsie with her? She watched in shock as everyone continued on with their conversation about American politics as though nothing out of the ordinary was happening. The sweaty foot was slowly making its way under her dress and up her calf. Disgusted and alarmed, Louise quickly and firmly stomped down on the offending foot with the heel of her shoe, and as if in a cartoon, Benjamin Guggenheim sprang out of his chair with a howl, knocking over his champagne into Mrs. Astor's cream of barley soup.

"Benjamin, what's gotten into you?" J. J. Astor exclaimed while trying to help his wife fish the crystal glass out of her broth.

Mr. Guggenheim flushed a deep rose color. Finally Louise wasn't the only one embarrassed. "Nothing, pardon me, just a bit of a foot cramp," he said, flustered, giving Louise a humiliated look as he sheepishly sat back down.

"How is dear Florette, Benjamin?" Mr. Baxter asked pointedly. "It's a shame she couldn't make it on this journey with us. Is she ill?"

"Florette is fine," Benjamin stammered.

OHMYGOD. This guy has a girlfriend?! Or a wife? A Florette! What a creep! Now she was starting to understand what "we" meant.

"Please give our best to your lovely wife. Have you sent her a telegraph yet? The technology on this ship is truly mind-boggling."

"You simply must come into the shop when we arrive in New York," Ida interrupted. "Isidor and I would love to dress you for your next event!" she said enthusiastically, seeming to sense the uncomfortable vibe and trying to change the subject.

"The shop?" Louise asked. Ida had found the one subject that could distract her from the horror of the last statement.

"Oh, you know, Macy's, our store," Ida answered, as though Louise should obviously know that already.

"You own Macy's?" Louise asked incredulously while buttering a warm dinner roll.

"Of course, sweetie. Did you hit your head this afternoon?" she asked, laughing.

"I suppose so," she answered. Brooke would be so jealous if she knew that Louise was having dinner with the owners of Macy's! She couldn't wait to tell her. She wondered if Brooke was at Macy's at that moment trying to find a new dress for the dance on Friday.

After that exchange, Louise hardly said a word during dinner. She was still totally hung up on the fact that the dashingly handsome man, the one who she had shared a boring but romantic walk with just a few hours earlier, was the biggest two-faced jerk she had ever met. Todd wasn't the most charming or gorgeous guy in the world, but at least he didn't have a secret double life! She was starting to wish she hadn't run away from him in the hall the other day. He deserved more than that.

When the rest of the table started talking about the Sherman Antitrust Act and the monopoly of Standard Oil, Louise tuned out. She hadn't reached that chapter yet in Miss Morris's history class and felt like she was stuck at a dinner party with her parents' older friends.

Her focus turned completely on the banquet of food that was practically spilling off the table. She had hardly eaten anything since her chicken salad sandwich that afternoon after swim practice. Did she really eat lunch in her Connecticut home earlier that day? It seemed like a lifetime ago. She was famished.

The next courses came out in rapid succession: ice-cold oysters that looked like slimy slugs but tasted like a burst of the sea, freshly caught salmon with cucumber and rich hollandaise sauce, filet mignon grilled to perfection and served with artichoke hearts and earthy mushrooms called truffles, lamb with mint sauce, creamed carrots, cold asparagus vinaigrette. Each course was delivered separately, by a constant parade of waiters. It was the most elaborate meal she had ever experienced; it was like going to the theater. These were by far the most scrumptious dishes Louise had ever tasted. Vegetables actually tasted delicious. Meat tasted tender and flavorful. There wasn't a drop of malt vinegar in any dish; so much for her mother's theories on English cooking. She ate with a greediness and hunger that she had never experienced in her previous life.

"Quite an appetite my niece has worked up," Mr. Baxter joked, trying to make light of an increasingly embarrassing situation, as the other ladies at the table delicately nibbled and picked at their food. He patted droplets of sweat from his head nervously with his damp pink pocket scarf. Louise had a feeling that Miss Baxter probably wouldn't be pigging out like this, but she couldn't help it.

"Ooh, I'm going to save this for Kitty," Mrs. Astor exclaimed, placing a lamb chop wrapped in a white cloth napkin into her silver beaded evening purse.

"My dear, that is absolutely disgusting," Mr. Astor said with a chuckle.

"Who's Kitty?" Louise asked, swallowing a mouthful of heavenly mashed potatoes.

"Silly, she's our Airedale. I'm sure you've met her before. How I love that dog," Mrs. Astor gushed.

"She eats better than I," Mr. Astor joked, taking a bite of his own food.

For dessert, yet another waiter rolled out a multitiered cart of sweets. There was no one to tell Louise that she should take only one little treat, that she had eaten enough already—only Mr. Baxter, who was staring in amazement at her display of consumption.

Louise had selected a piece of decadent chocolate cake, which had been prominently displayed on the top shelf of the cart. Shoveling a heaping spoonful into her mouth, she discovered it had a warm and gooey center that tasted like brownie batter. It was perfectly accompanied by a scoop of silky vanilla-bean ice cream. With each bite, Louise's corset was getting tighter and more constricting. How did women eat in these things?

Spooning up the last succulent bit of chocolate goo, she

reluctantly acknowledged that her body was in intense pain. She leaned back in her chair and rested her hands on her stiff corseted belly. The rest of the table was still eyeing her suspiciously, although pretending to be engrossed in their personal conversations.

Louise opened up her gold mesh evening purse to reapply Miss Baxter's glamorous lipstick. She would have to find a way to sneak a tube of this back to Connecticut with her. It was the perfect shade of movie-star matte red. The texture was thick and creamy, and they didn't make anything like it anymore.

Fishing around the deceptively cavernous clutch, she pulled out a crumpled-up piece of cardstock. Louise unfolded the balled-up piece of paper.

Say what?! I'm where?!

"OHMUHGOD we are on the *Titanic*?" Louise screamed in panic, holding up the piece of paper. The table got quiet, and all eyes stared directly at her. Then, in unison, everyone burst out laughing, like it was the most hilarious joke they had ever heard.

"Of course we are, my dear. What an amazing actress she is, isn't she?" Mr. Baxter exclaimed. "I'm glad I signed her when I did!" He took another large gulp of his champagne.

"You are an odd bird," Benjamin Guggenheim chided through his laughter.

And you are a cheating creep, Louise wanted to scream back at him. But she didn't, because it hardly seemed important anymore, considering this newest and extremely disturbing revelation. With shaking hands, she dropped the boarding pass onto the food-stained tablecloth.

"May I be excused?" Louise asked, not forgetting her manners in even the most dire of circumstances. "There's something I need to take care of." Shakily, she got up from her seat, still in shock that she had failed to realize she was a passenger on the most infamous doomed ship in history. Without waiting for a response, she unstrapped herself from Miss Baxter's pinching high heels and hurriedly walked barefoot toward the captain's table.

Halfway across the dining room, she heard Mr. Baxter calling out, "Alice! Where are you going? We haven't had the cheese course yet...." But Louise didn't turn around. She was sick of playing the role of Miss Baxter, and now she was scared. She marched straight ahead, determined to speak with the captain. This wasn't a game anymore. She needed to get home.

CHAPTER 25

The captain's cheeks were rosy from drink, and he had the entire table enraptured by an anecdote he was telling. When Louise walked up to the table, he stopped mid sentence and greeted her warmly.

"Excuse me, Captain Smith, I'm sorry to interrupt," she began hesitantly.

"Miss Baxter, not at all! It's wonderful to see you looking much more vivacious. How are you feeling?" he asked enthusiastically.

"I'm fine, sir," Louise replied slowly, not sure how to phrase what she had intended to say now that all eyes were on her.

"But I need to speak with you privately; it's rather urgent."

"Let me get you a seat," he gestured. "I'm sure nothing can be that pressing on such a gorgeous night as this. And you'll have to pry me away from this chocolate soufflé," he added, pointing to the china plate on which sat his half-eaten dessert.

"Have you met my lovely wife, Eleanor?" the captain inquired. Mrs. Smith smiled at Louise with a vapid expression. She was an attractive enough older lady with silver chin-length hair and thin lips who looked a lot like the librarian at Louise's school.

"And my first officer," the captain continued, "William Murdoch. You two met this afternoon."

"Yes," Louise said impatiently, "but—"

"Please, do join us," Mrs. Smith chimed in. "Edward was telling me that you had quite a scare this afternoon."

"I'm fine," Louise repeated, a bit more firmly. "But I really do need to speak with you, or else no one will be fine."

"Dear, whatever are you talking about? Please sit down, have some tea. You're getting quite flushed," Mrs. Smith remarked calmly.

Almost on cue, Louise felt the warmth spreading up her neck to her cheeks. "I don't have time to sit down. I need you to come with me. We need to change the direction the boat is headed," Louise said as she looked intently at the captain.

"Change our course?" the captain responded in disbelief.

"The *Titanic* is going to hit an iceberg. I'm not sure when, but we can't have much time left." As Louise said this, her voice was getting louder and more hysterical. Passengers at nearby tables turned their heads to see what the commotion was about.

"Miss Baxter, please lower your voice. What's gotten into you?" he asked, his voice now stern.

"I need you to listen to me. I can't explain now, but you need to trust me. We are going to crash. I'm sure of it," Louise pleaded.

"Believe me, Miss Baxter, as your captain, I am telling you that we are safe. We are *not* going to collide with an iceberg. The *Titanic* is unsinkable," he replied confidently. "Now if you don't sit down, you are going to alarm the other passengers."

"Yes, please, have a seat," Mrs. Smith parroted. "It's probably just nerves. You're still recovering from this afternoon." She spoke without losing her plastered-on smile, while the rest of her face remained frozen and expressionless. *Did they already have Botox in 1912?* Louise couldn't help wondering at that moment.

Then she got back into focus. "I'm fine!" she exploded, feeling her ears getting hot in anger. Why wouldn't they listen to her? Why were they dismissing her like this? "We need to change direction. We need to stop, or thousands of people will die. I know it's going to happen. It's history."

"We are staying the course," Captain Smith said as he rose to his feet.

"If you want to go down in history as the captain of a sinking ship..." Louise threatened, not able to control her temper anymore.

By this point, they were attracting quite a bit of attention from nearby tables. The orchestra conductor was doing his best to drown out the commotion with crescendos of music. The first officer, a ruddy older man with an intense gaze, had also risen to his feet. He was stealthily making his way around the table toward Louise.

"Why don't we get Dr. Hastings? He'll be able to give you something to calm your nerves," First Officer Murdoch said in a firm tone. "It's normal for a woman to become frightened on a ship."

"I sometimes get scared, too," Mrs. Smith added. "We delicate females simply can't help it."

"But what I can't have," the captain continued, interrupting his wife, "is you scaring the other passengers with this nonsense. Do you know how quickly this irrational fear can spread?"

While he said this, the burly first officer had almost reached Louise, who was slowly starting to back away from the table as she realized the trouble she was in. He reached out to grab her by the arm, and Louise took off running, in her bare feet, through the dining room.

As she ran, she saw Dr. Hastings unfolding himself from his chair. His two dinner companions jumped to their feet.

"Alice! Where are you running to?" a befuddled Mr. Baxter called out across the room.

She didn't stop to answer, nor did she turn around to see if First Officer Murdoch and Dr. Hastings were chasing her. She just ran as fast as was possible for a lady in a rock-hard corset.

Louise exited the dining room, flew back up the Grand Staircase, elbowed her way past several stunned passengers, turned down a long, maroon-carpeted hallway, up a short flight of stairs, and finally burst out into the open air on the upper deck.

Shaking, she took in huge gulps of the fresh sea air. She turned around slowly, half expecting to see that she had been followed, but no one was there. The wind was biting, and she hugged her bare arms around her body.

Louise stood at the railing and looked out at the expansive sea. For the first time in her life, the sight of water didn't fill her with a feeling of freedom and excitement. She felt quite the opposite: trapped. She was stuck on a sinking ship in a life and body that weren't hers.

Looking up at the infinite, starry night, Louise couldn't help but wonder if her mother was looking up at that same sky, worried that she hadn't come home for supper. Were there really a hundred years separating them? She bit her lip so that she wouldn't cry. She needed to keep a clear head.

She began twirling her hair and pacing the deck to keep warm. Perhaps she had been naïve in believing that the

captain would listen to her. But she could not give up. There must be someone else in the crew who would believe her. She needed to find the navigation room. If she could stall the boat for only a moment, or veer it off course by the slightest degree, maybe the disaster could be averted.

Louise continued twirling and pacing and was completely lost in her own thoughts when she walked directly into the skeletal frame of Dr. Hastings.

CHAPTER 26

"Miss Baxter, what a pleasant surprise," the doctor hissed. Louise looked around frantically for another passenger who could help her, but the deck was deserted.

"Do you really think you should be outside without a wrap in your condition? You'll catch your death." He grabbed her upper arm in a viselike grip. "I'll be happy to escort you back to your stateroom."

Louise tried to protest, but the doctor would not let her go. "Please let go of my arm, Doctor. The fresh air will do me good," she pleaded.

"No, Miss Baxter. As your doctor, I insist. You must come inside at once." He began to pull her toward the ship door. He was strong, despite his advanced age and bony frame.

Louise tried to keep her feet firmly planted on the deck but managed only to get a splinter in her right heel as she was dragged across the wooden planks. "I have explicit orders from the captain to make sure that you are taken directly to your room and then given something to calm your nerves," the doctor declared. "We can't have a hysterical woman upsetting the other passengers."

He pushed her roughly through the door and back into the ship, still refusing to loosen his iron-tight grip.

"You're hurting me," Louise growled through clenched teeth. Dr. Hastings ignored her pleas and continued to forcefully lead her through the empty hallways. They made a sharp turn and, out of the corner of her eye, Louise thought she saw two women in wide-brimmed hats at the end of the corridor. Before she could call out for help, they darted around the next corner.

With a sudden movement, Dr. Hastings pushed her into a dark room. Without giving her eyes time to adjust, he switched on the electric lights, and Louise saw that she was back in her stateroom. "Miss Baxter, as your doctor, I am ordering you to rest." He still had her by the arm and was dragging her over to the wooden four-poster bed.

Louise decided to change her strategy and reluctantly climbed up into the bed. Perhaps she could pretend to be asleep and then break out and continue on her mission.

"Where is Uncle Baxter? Where is Anna?" Louise asked, hoping they would walk into the room at any moment.

"They are in their respective dining rooms. You ran out

before the entertainment. And thanks to your antics, I am now missing my poker game," Dr. Hastings responded huffily.

"I'd like to see them," she demanded, trying to sound braver than she felt. "Why don't you go find them for me?"

"Oh, they'll be back soon. However, you will most certainly be asleep by then. The captain requested that I give you something to be sure of that."

"Oh no, I'm quite sleepy already, no need for any sleeping medicines," Louise tried to speak slowly and in a casual tone, but she was starting to panic.

Dr. Hastings paid her no attention as he rummaged through his black leather medicine bag. She wondered nervously if he was looking for sleeping pills. She made a quick plan to hide them under her tongue and spit the tablets out later. Louise let out an exaggerated yawn. "Wow, am I tired," she lied.

Dr. Hastings grunted triumphantly. He had found what he was looking for. "Now you see, Miss Baxter, I am not one who disobeys my captain's orders." He carefully extracted a syringe with what had to be a three-inch-long pricker. He tested it, and a little squirt of clear liquid shot out the tip. "Come now, this won't hurt at all."

"No!" Louise screamed. "Don't you dare stick me with that!"

"It's to help you sleep through the night," he explained in a fake soothing voice. "All natural. A vitamin shot." He was inching toward the bed with the syringe poised in his right hand.

"Don't touch me!" Louise shouted again. But the doctor ignored her cries.

She scurried to the other side of the bed, trying to escape, but the doctor's reflexes were too sharp. He grabbed her by the ankle, and without a moment's hesitation, jabbed the needle into the top of her exposed left foot.

Louise let out a high-pitched scream of pain and shock. She turned to look into the doctor's remorseless black eyes, and within a few moments, everything else in the room turned into that same bottomless black.

CHAPTER 27

That night Louise had the most extraordinary dreams.

She dreamed she was covered in a thick blanket of darkness. She was in a cave that was so deep and so black that she didn't know how she would ever return to the world above the earth. Her legs felt like lead weights, anchoring her to this lower and darker world.

"Open your eyes, open your eyes," a woman's voice hissed. The raspy voice sounded miles away.

"Open your eyes," the distant voice said more urgently. Louise's eyelids were so heavy, how could she possibly open them? What if she obeyed the voice and was to awaken into another layer of dream? What if she could open her eyes and still be dreaming?

"Open your eyes." The voice was getting closer and stronger. Louise had to obey; she didn't have a choice anymore.

She was immediately blinded by a burst of color, like a fiery red cloud.

"Louise," the voice whispered, "the time is near. You must save yourself. History cannot be rewritten, but the dress will prevail." Louise saw a flash of gold and an image of a black poodle dangling in the red cloud. She could no longer fight the utter heaviness of her eyelids, and her weighted feet plummeted her back down into the darkness below.

The cave was filling up quickly with rushing water. The cold water rapidly rose up past her ankles and her knees. The water was tickling her thighs. She tried screaming but, like in all of her most terrifying nightmares, no sound came out of her mouth. The only sound was the roar of the water pouring into the black cave. The icy wetness had reached her belly button, and Louise felt a stabbing pain in her stomach. The water level was quickly moving up to her chest. She heard two distinct female voices yelling, but she was too far away to make out the words.

She bolted upright in bed. An evening dress was clinging to her like another layer of skin. She anxiously glanced around the room to get her bearings. Now she could never be sure where she would wake up. The room was dimly lit, but Louise recognized it immediately as Miss Baxter's stateroom.

How she wished that she would wake up in her familiar

bedroom under her grandmother's handsewn patchwork quilt. She hoped this was all a long, awful nightmare.

"Miss Baxter? Are you all right?" Anna asked eagerly as she came over to the bed.

"No, I'm not," Louise croaked, her throat parched. "I just had the most horrible nightmare. And then I woke up, and I'm in the middle of an even worse nightmare. . . ." She paused. "Anna, are you okay?" A terrified look was spreading across her friend's face. "What's wrong? You look like you've seen a ghost."

Even in the dimly lit room, Louise could see Anna's pallid complexion and trembling bottom lip.

"I'm not sure," Anna said hesitantly. "I think I may have."

CHAPTER 28

"Go on," Louise urged, propping herself up on her elbows as Anna sat down at the foot of the bed.

"I don't know, maybe I didn't see anything," Anna stuttered. "I feel like I'm losing my mind. Please, forget I said anything." Her gaze was darting around the room, as though she expected something or someone to jump out of the shadows.

"No," Louise blurted. "You have to tell me. I'll believe you!"

"Well, ma'am," her friend began slowly. "Last night when I returned from dinner...I was sleeping right over here on the sofa to keep an eye on you," Anna said as she gestured to a nearby Victorian couch made up with pillows and blankets. "Oh, Miss Baxter, we were all worried sick. I hear you caused quite a stir in the dining room last evening, that you told Captain Smith the *Titanic* was going to sink—"

"It is," Louise interrupted, "but what happened?"

"That's impossible. There has never been a more magnificent or sturdy boat to cross the ocean."

"What happened next?" Louise asked, trying to get back to the story, hoping it would give her some clue as to how to get off the boat.

"Well, I was asleep right here on this sofa," she began again hesitantly.

"I know, I know," Louise said as she nodded vigorously.

"And in the middle of the night, I heard strange voices, so I woke up out of a deep sleep. And then I saw them." Anna got up and started pacing the room nervously.

"Saw who?" Louise asked.

"There were two women hovering over your bed, whispering things to you. When I called out in fright, they disappeared—vanished into thin air. Oh, it's impossible. Hail Mary." Anna made the sign of the cross over her body.

"No, Anna, I believe you! What did they say?" Louise asked urgently, now sitting fully upright in the bed.

"I couldn't make out the words they were saying. They were leaning over you, speaking softly into your ear," Anna recounted.

"What did they look like?"

"One of them was very tall with wild red hair. The other was much shorter with brown hair, and she had her hands placed over your stomach."

"Marla and Glenda!" Louise said with a gasp. "It must be." Instinctively, she placed her hands on her belly, still somewhat experiencing the gnawing pain in her stomach that she had felt in her dream. How did the women know that? Were they the cause of it?

"They were right here, and then they literally vanished." Anna was clearly shaken. But Louise felt vindicated: She wasn't crazy.

"Anna, we need to find those women," Louise whispered loudly, eyes flashing.

"The witches?" Anna asked, scared. She began furiously making up the sofa bed where she had slept the night before. It reminded Louise of her mother, who would also tidy up when she got nervous.

"Yes, it's the only way for me to get back to my normal life in Connecticut. And they can save you, too. This boat is doomed!"

"Connecticut?" Anna repeated, confused. "And what do you mean this boat is doomed?"

"The *Titanic* is going to sink," Louise replied bluntly, her eyes getting hot with held-back tears.

"Why do you keep saying that?" Anna questioned. "Everyone says it's unsinkable...."

"I guess nothing is indestructible," Louise concluded. "Ships, planes, nations, presidents. You would never believe me if I told you what was going to happen in the next one hundred years."

"How would *you* know what the future holds, Miss Baxter?" Anna asked hysterically, refolding the wool blanket she had in her hands.

"Anna, I didn't say anything before, because it sounds crazy, but I'm not Miss Baxter. And I'm not an actress. The truth is my name is Louise, and I'm from Connecticut. It's a state in America. One of the last things I remember is that it was 2011, and I was learning about the *Titanic* disaster in my history class." Suddenly Louise wished she had paid a little more attention to Miss Morris's lecture.

Anna stopped fluffing the pillows and made the sign of the cross over her body again. Apparently she had reconnected with her religion sometime over the course of the night.

"You're not the real Miss Baxter?" she asked incredulously. "But you look exactly like Miss Baxter. How could you possibly be anyone else?" Anna walked over to the bed and gave her a thorough once-over.

"I don't know," Louise replied, frustrated, throwing her hands in the air in a helpless shrug. "It seems impossible, but I swear, I'm not her."

Anna still didn't look convinced.

"Would Miss Baxter do this?" Louise asked, crossing her eyes, sticking out her tongue.

Anna giggled, despite her extreme state of fear. "Certainly not. Perhaps Dr. Hastings gave you too strong a dose of that sleeping medicine."

"Wait, come over here," Louise commanded in a loud whisper, as she walked toward a gilded mirror hanging on the opposite wall. Anna needed to see her as Louise, and words would never convince her otherwise. Anna gave her a quizzical look but followed anyway. With great trepidation, Louise stepped in front of it, her head lowered—afraid of whom she would see.

She had spent her entire life wishing that something in her appearance would be different—that her hair would grow in like fifties starlet Elizabeth Taylor's perfectly smooth brunette waves or that the mosquito bites on her chest would develop into real breasts so she could finally wear a bra like every other girl in the seventh grade. It took her by surprise that now all she wanted was to look exactly as she was. She needed to recognize herself.

Looking directly into the mirror, Louise once again saw herself for who she truly was—a skinny, twelve-year-old girl with braces. For the first time since this whole adventure began, she burst into tears—hot tears of exhaustion and happiness at seeing the first familiar face she had recognized all day.

Stunned, Anna gasped, crossed herself, and stared silently

into the gilded mirror. Finally she said in absolute horror, "What do you have on your teeth?"

Louise laughed and wiped her tear-streaked cheeks and running nose with the back of her arm. "Be grateful you were born when you were. You're lucky they hadn't invented these orthodontic torture devices yet."

Anna sat down shakily on the edge of the sofa. It was too much for her to handle. "*Who are you?*"

"My name is Louise Lambert. I'm from Fairview, Connecticut. I was born in 1999, and I'm twelve years old." As she spoke, she felt her voice grow stronger, more confident. *Wow, that felt really good,* she thought with a smile. It was an overwhelming moment. She knew she was finally ready to be Louise again. But time was running out, and she needed to find an answer quickly.

CHAPTER 29

Louise climbed up and sat on the edge of the puffy feather-bed; her feet didn't even touch the floor. She wanted to tell Anna everything she remembered from Miss Morris about the *Titanic*. Unfortunately, thanks to her teacher's monotonous lecturing style, it wasn't all that much.

"If I had to end up on the *Titanic*, I wish a young Leo was on board," she said jokingly, thinking about the romantic epic movie that was made a few years before she was born. She had seen it recently, when she was home sick with a cold.

"Who?" Anna asked, understandably, considering Leonardo DiCaprio wasn't exactly alive in 1912.

"Never mind, I guess you had to be there," Louise said, snapping back into focus. "The basic story is that one night this very fancy boat named *Titanic* collides with an iceberg and sinks. I know this is incredibly frightening to hear, but it really happened. Do you believe me?"

"I wish I didn't." Anna put her hand to her mouth, pausing to take it all in. "But after seeing your image in the mirror, I suppose I have to believe anything at this point. How did you manage to make yourself look like Miss Baxter to everyone else and do such a convincing job of impersonating her?"

"Honestly, I don't know," Louise confessed. "It's totally crazy that everyone thinks I look like her. But I guess I've been preparing for this role all my life."

"Incredible," Anna said as she shook her head, dumb-founded. "I could swear I was talking to the real Miss Baxter. This is too bizarre. So...so...if you are Louise Lambert... where is Miss Baxter?"

"I have no idea." Louise hadn't even begun to ponder this angle of the story when suddenly they were startled by a loud snoring noise coming from the adjacent suite.

"Mr. Baxter!" she exclaimed in a loud whisper, having forgotten about him for a moment. "I'll explain everything I can later, but we need to get out of here before he wakes up. Or else we'll both have a lot of explaining to do, and we must escape."

"Don't worry, he could sleep through a shipwreck. Oops," Anna said with a gasp, blushing a deep crimson, embarrassed by her ominous choice of words.

"Quickly. Let's get out of here," Louise urged, jumping down from the bed.

"First, you should put on some dry clothes," Anna advised

in a motherly tone. Louise looked down. She was still wearing the navy blue beaded evening dress. It was now damp and clinging from her panicky sweat.

"Does Miss Baxter own any jeans?" Louise asked hopefully.

"Jeans?" Anna responded in disbelief. "You mean the denim overalls that the railroad workers wear?"

"Oh, never mind." Louise dreaded putting on another dress. She missed her own limited wardrobe back home. Trying to escape from this ship would be much easier in pants.

"Where are you going, ladies?"

The girls jumped. Mr. Baxter was standing in the doorway of the sitting room wearing a pair of pink silk pajamas with red piping and a sleeping mask dangling around his neck. His handlebar mustache was a little askew.

"Uncle Baxter," Louise cooed, instantly switching back to her Miss Baxter character. She hoped she could still pull off this façade, even though all she could think about was getting off the boat as quickly as possible.

Mr. Baxter removed a gold tassel earplug from his left ear.

"Uncle Baxter," she repeated, this time fluttering her eyelashes like an overcaffeinated butterfly. "I couldn't sleep, so Anna is going to fetch me some warm milk and honey." That was her mother's cure for insomnia. Louise hoped it was a really old recipe.

Mr. Baxter looked at both girls sleepily.

"Uncle Baxter," she piped up for the third time. "Go back to bed. You need your beauty sleep."

Too confused and tired to argue, Mr. Baxter padded back into his sleeping quarters.

"Good morning and good night, ladies," he mumbled drowsily, shutting the antique oak French doors behind him.

The girls exchanged a relieved look. Very quietly but quickly, Anna snuck around the suite, gathering some fresh clothes for Louise. Louise quickly changed into the simple wool dress and brown button-up leather boots that Anna had lent her.

Together, they tiptoed out of the room and gently shut the door behind them before running as fast as they could down the hall.

CHAPTER 30

"We have to be careful. We need to stay away from Captain Smith and Dr. Hastings at all costs," Louise whispered as they ran as quietly as possible along the deserted and dimly lit hallway.

Anna nodded. "But where exactly are we going?"

"I don't know. I want to get a clear map of the ship in my head. Do you know your way around?" From what she had seen, there seemed to be miles of passageways that all looked remarkably similar. "Do you know where the navigation room is?" Louise asked more specifically.

"Yes, I do," Anna said as she nodded vigorously. "Although it's off limits to passengers; we're not allowed up there."

"That's where we need to go!" Louise decided. "There must be someone there who will believe us and change course."

"Captain Smith is a very powerful man," Anna interrupted, grabbing her arm. "It's not going to be easy to find someone who will disobey his orders. Especially if the new orders are coming from two women."

Louise sighed, feeling another surge of panic. She kept forgetting that in 1912 women didn't even have the right to vote, and that her opinion might be ignored simply because it came from a female voice. "Maybe we should first find Glenda and Marla. If you saw them and Lucy saw them, then they must be on the *Titanic* with us...."

"The witches?" Anna trembled, interrupting Louise's train of thought.

"I'm afraid it might be the only way."

"I think we should go with the first plan," Anna said nervously. "I mean, how will we know it won't work if we don't even try? And I know someone who might help us."

"Who?" Louise asked.

"Oh...just some boy," Anna replied quickly.

"You lead the way," Louise ordered. "We can use all the help we can get."

"This way," Anna said as she motioned for Louise to follow her. They scurried in a thoughtful silence until they reached the outer deck and then headed toward the bow of the ship. Anna led them past a group of ladies lounging on wooden deck chairs huddled under white blankets embroidered with the White Star insignia, sipping hot toddies and enjoying the morning sun.

Louise looked up and saw several wooden lifeboats suspended with ropes and cables overhead. Maybe she and Anna could urge the ladies to come with them and get one down and escape now before the *Titanic* hit the iceberg.

Staring up at the lifeboats, Louise was suddenly transported back to her history class. She could hear Miss Morris's dull but informative voice inside her head. "The fatal flaw of the *Titanic* was that it did not contain nearly enough lifeboats for its two thousand passengers. To compound this fact, the boats were frantically lowered into the sea half empty, and precious lifesaving seats were left vacant."

How could Louise justify stealing a boat for a handful of people when there already weren't enough seats for every passenger? And, she realized, the chances of convincing these ladies to put down their steaming drinks to get into a small lifeboat in the middle of the freezing cold Atlantic Ocean was pretty unlikely. As badly as she wanted to get off the ship, she realized that she wasn't willing to save herself at the expense of so many others.

"We're almost at the bridge," Anna said in between breaths to Louise.

"The bridge?"

"That's the place where the ship is navigated from."

"Perfect. You lead the way."

Anna continued to lead them hurriedly down the deck and

then stopped suddenly at a door that read PRIVATE—DO NOT ENTER.

"Here we are," she announced, looking at Louise ominously.

Louise glanced around. The coast was clear. The two girls opened the forbidden door and slipped inside.

CHAPTER 31

"Follow me," Anna whispered, grabbing on to a suspended ladder and hoisting herself up with ease. "It's sturdy. Don't worry," she added as she climbed up.

Louise hitched up her skirt, curious as to how Anna knew so much about this, and followed her friend up the dark wooden ladder. She climbed over the top rung into what she realized must be the navigation room. Maps and sea charts were hanging on the walls and spread out over every available flat surface.

"What are you ladies doing? Passengers are not allowed in here!" a voice boomed from somewhere behind them.

Startled, Louise and Anna spun around to find a young crew member with cropped blond hair wearing a navy White Star Line uniform.

"Anna, is that you?" The crew member's voice suddenly lowered. "What did you bring her up here for? Now I'll get in a heap of trouble."

It seemed that Anna did, in fact, have a secret crush, Louise immediately realized. A really cute secret crush.

"She won't get you into trouble, Christopher," Anna said as she took his hand. "I promise." She gave him a quick kiss on the cheek. "But I need you to help us out." Christopher blushed a deep red and looked worriedly at Louise, or rather Miss Baxter.

He was definitely good-looking: sixteen, maybe seventeen years old, tan, very short sun-bleached hair, sky blue eyes. Actually he was more Brooke's type, Louise thought, instantly missing her best friend more than ever. She couldn't help but wonder if she would ever see Brooke again.

"I'll try. But you really shouldn't be in here. If Captain Smith comes up, that will be the end of it—and my job."

"Don't worry. I won't let that happen," Louise interrupted, rationalizing that it would be better to be fired than dead.

"It's a bit complicated to explain," Anna began, choosing her words carefully, "but let's just say that Miss Baxter has had a premonition that the *Titanic* is going to hit an iceberg and sink." She grabbed Christopher's hand tighter as she spoke. "We need you to change the course of the ship, only by the slightest degree, or else we—"

"What?" Christopher interrupted, pulling his hand away. "Anna, have you lost your mind?"

"Please," Louise pleaded. "You must believe us!"

"You want me to disobey my captain's orders and lose my job because of a *premonition*?" His clear blue eyes opened wide in disbelief. "I will do you a favor and not tell the captain you were up here, but that's all I'll do." He put his hands up, backing away from the girls.

"You'll do nothing of the sort!" Louise and Anna spun around and came face-to-face with a very angry Dr. Hastings. He shut the door behind him and walked briskly over to Louise. "This has gone far enough," he growled, grabbing her by the wrist. "Now you've become a danger, not only to yourself but to the other twenty-two hundred passengers who are on this ship with you."

"Dr. Hastings, Christopher, you both need to listen to me! I am a respected actress, a public figure...and if the press hears that you even attempted to lay one finger on me..." Louise said as she extracted her wrist from Dr. Hastings's loosening grip. This was by far her most impressive, Oscar-worthy Miss Baxter performance. "Well, the public would be outraged...." Louise trailed off, noticing that Christopher suddenly looked very scared. Was she doing *that* good of a job? Anything to get off this boat!

Christopher raised his right hand and pointed at the wall across from Louise. He was ruining her plea; what could it be? She looked over at Anna, who had turned a ghastly shade of pale.

Louise turned to the left, following Christopher's terrified expression and pointing index finger. And what she saw shocked even her. It was herself, twelve and awkward, dressed in a drab, old-fashioned costume, being reflected off the large circular mirror hanging on the opposite wall. She felt her façade crumble. In the middle of her most important performance, she was being exposed for who she truly was.

"Witches!" Dr. Hastings said with a snarl, his bottom lip trembling. "Good God Almighty, we're dealing with witches."

Louise and Anna slowly started backing away.

"You're seeing things, Doctor," Louise said cleverly, walking backward toward the captain's wheel.

"Oh no, I'm not. I may be a man of medicine, but I know a witch when I see one."

Before the evil doctor could drag her away, Louise frantically reached out, grabbed the massive wooden steering wheel, and gave it a hard yank. She could have sworn she felt the boat jerk ever so slightly to the right.

"Stay the course!" Dr. Hastings bellowed as Christopher rushed to the wheel.

"Latitude, forty-one degrees, north, longitude, fifty degrees, west," Christopher replied automatically.

Within minutes, the *Titanic* was back on its predestined route.

But maybe it was enough? Louise thought frantically, as

Dr. Hastings tightened his grip on her and roughly pushed her toward the door. *Have I just rewritten history?*

"We are going to put you where you won't be able to cause any more trouble, somewhere very quiet and dark. Where no one will be able to hear your hysterical nonsense. You have put all of our lives in danger with such theatrics. I need to alert the captain as to who or what we're dealing with here," he said gruffly.

"No, Doctor!" Louise screamed. "I am not the one who is putting our lives in danger. But I suppose history will be the judge of that!"

Louise and Anna were pushed roughly into a claustrophobically tiny broom closet off the navigation room. The door swung shut behind them with a sickening slam.

CHAPTER 32

"What are we going to do?" Anna sobbed, her head in her hands. They'd been sitting on wooden milk crates in a stunned silence for what seemed like an eternity.

The windowless room was crowded with boxes and brooms and illuminated by one flickering bulb. Louise began furiously twirling her hair. She did not like to be locked in small spaces for indefinite periods of time. Particularly when on a ship that was probably going to collide with an iceberg before the day was over. She paced the perimeter of her prison like a caged animal. When she had sufficiently exhausted herself from panic and fury, she sat down on an overturned, splintery crate next to Anna.

"I don't know what we're going to do.... I never liked mirrors. I guess they might end up being my downfall after all," Louise joked feebly. They were both quiet for a minute.

"Do you have a bobby pin?" She suddenly had an idea. In her Nancy Drew books, all that seemed to be required to spring open a lock was a bobby pin or a credit card. And she had a feeling Anna wouldn't have an AmEx on her.

Anna fished around in her tousled blonde bun for a moment and triumphantly pulled out an old-fashioned hairpin.

"Tell me again about Miss Baxter," Louise requested, trying to calm Anna down while she straightened out the U-shaped tool.

"Well, you are, I mean, Miss Baxter is, very beautiful," Anna answered, wiping her nose with her dress sleeve.

"I saw her photograph," Louise said and then distracted herself for a moment with a sigh. The pin was taking a while to straighten. "She looked like a gorgeous movie star."

"You are. I mean, Miss Baxter is an actress. She's quite talented. I've seen almost all of her theater performances and moving pictures."

"When I look in the mirror, I see myself; I'm twelve, not some glamorous woman," Louise explained. "I can't see Miss Baxter. And even though it was fun for a little while, I don't want her to be me. I miss me! That sounds so weird."

"It's so strange." Anna had been listening intently. "When I look at you now, you are Miss Baxter. You are quite stunning."

"She must have a wonderful life," Louise mused, standing

up from her makeshift seat and heading over to the doorknob to try her new tool.

"I suppose," Anna said hesitantly.

"She doesn't?" Louise asked, surprised by her friend's tone.

"I'm not quite certain. I never really could get to know her. She seems a little sad to me, a little distant. She is a very private person."

"Hmm..." Louise mused, focusing her attention on picking the lock, a task she had never done before in her life.

"For instance," Anna started, "we would never be having this conversation if you were the real Miss Baxter."

"That's really sad," Louise said, jiggling the pin in the lock, not exactly sure what she was doing but determined to make it work.

"I think *she* was sad," Anna replied. "Once I walked into her dressing room and caught her by surprise. She was all dressed up in this beautiful pink evening gown. In fact, it was the same gown you were wearing when you fainted on the A Deck. And even though it was an ordinary Sunday afternoon, she was made up as if for a gala. She had music playing on the Victrola and was twirling around in this dress, looking absolutely carefree and lovely. I didn't want to spoil the moment. But when she finally saw me standing in the doorway, she stopped and got very angry. She yelled at me for not announcing myself. I felt as though I had seen too much."

"What do you mean?" Louise asked. She jerked the pin to the right and heard a clicking sound. Eagerly she turned the knob. It didn't budge. "Darn," Louise cursed under her breath.

"I think she longs for something she isn't getting in her life. Something more. Of course she would never tell me any of this. I don't think she confides in anyone."

"How awful. I guess there are a few things we actually do have in common." Louise was surprisingly moved by Anna's story. If she ever saw Brooke again, she would have to tell her absolutely everything. Not that she would *ever* believe this.

"I guess everyone wants to be leading another, more glamorous, more exciting life," Louise mused. "The life you imagine that you'll be living once your real life begins. Do you think that exists, Anna?"

"Do I think what exists?" Anna asked, seemingly confused.

Louise didn't have time to explain. They were interrupted by some muffled shouts and a key scratching in the lock. The door swiftly swung open, letting in a stream of light. Louise shielded her eyes and palmed the hairpin. Captain Smith stood in the doorway holding a large ring of keys while Dr. Hastings hovered over his shoulder like a dark shadow.

"How dare you lock my niece and her maid up in this cell?" Mr. Baxter shouted, pushing his way past the other men, his round face purple with rage. "My dear, are you hurt?" he asked, without giving Louise a moment to answer. "You have locked them in here like common criminals. Like animals! We are first-class passengers. I would have been worried sick looking for them, had one of your decent crew members not alerted me to the situation!" Mr. Baxter shouted, a sheepish Christopher standing a few feet behind him.

"But she's not Miss Baxter. She's a witch pretending to be her. I would bet my reputation on it!" Dr. Hastings protested.

"A witch? Have you absolutely lost your mind?" Captain Smith asked.

"I know it sounds crazy, but I can prove it. Look in the mirror!" Dr. Hastings shouted while pointing to where the mirror had been.

"What mirror?" Mr. Baxter asked as he looked at what was now just a bare white wall. "Perhaps you should prescribe something to rid yourself of these hallucinations."

Louise was stunned. Someone had removed the mirror. She turned to see Anna smiling, her gaze cast shyly down toward the floor.

Christopher's face had grown an even deeper shade of red. He had saved them! He must have done it for Anna, Louise realized. And judging by the smile on Anna's face, she knew it, too.

"But it was hanging there before," Dr. Hastings stammered, pointing his long crooked finger. "I saw it."

"Oh, go eat some prunes," Mr. Baxter answered in disgust.

"I am so sorry, Miss Baxter. Please accept my humblest apologies. Anything I can do to make up for this," Captain Smith said, embarrassed.

"Let me find another mirror. I swear I can prove it," the doctor pleaded desperately.

"I don't want to hear it!" Mr. Baxter roared, his veins bulging out of his neck. "And if you so much as come within a hundred meters of Miss Baxter or Miss Hard, I will make sure that you never practice medicine again. Do I make myself clear?"

"Crystal clear," the doctor seethed through clenched teeth, giving Louise a searing look.

Louise returned the glare.

"Well, there is one thing you can do for me," she said as she turned to the captain.

"Anything. A bottle of our finest champagne, perhaps?"

"She's only seventeen!" Mr. Baxter practically exploded. "She doesn't drink!"

"I would like for you to change the course of the ship," Louise said bluntly. "We are going to hit an iceberg if we continue on this path."

"Not this again!" Captain Smith said as he threw his hands up in frustration.

"Please excuse her," Mr. Baxter interrupted. "She has been

locked in a broom closet for God knows how long and doesn't know what she's saying."

Mr. Baxter took Louise by the hand and hastily escorted her and Anna out of the navigation room and into the fresh sea air. It was a particularly chilly evening, and the sun had already begun to set. He led them back to the stateroom in silence, rushing them through the maze of corridors, dragging Louise by the hand, with Anna following close behind.

"I'm coming," Louise said, annoyed, shaking off Mr. Baxter's hand. She didn't want to be trapped back in the stateroom, either. They needed help. She desperately needed to find Marla and Glenda!

When they arrived at their door, Mr. Baxter pulled a gold pocket watch from his tweed vest. "Well, at least we haven't missed supper. We are expected in the à la carte dining room in half an hour. Why, what in heavens are you wearing?" he asked, looking Louise over with a puzzled and disapproving gaze. Louise glanced down at her coarse, shapeless dress and shrugged.

"Uncle Baxter, I assume Anna will be dining with us tonight? As she has suffered through this horrible ordeal with me."

"Whatever you wish, my dear. I have no objection," he said, sounding exhausted.

"Let's not mention this unfortunate incident again," he

197

added, unlocking the room and then ushering them inside. "I'd rather forget about all of this. Understood?"

"I'm going to get dressed for dinner," Louise said, trying to sound relaxed as she walked through the bedroom and sitting room and into the dressing room. She had already begun to think of the next plan.

"I'll be there in a moment to help you with your corset," Anna called after her.

Louise closed the closet door behind her and was surprised to find some unexpected visitors.

CHAPTER 33

"How did you get in here?" she asked excitedly.

"We know when we're needed. Darling, don't you look fabulous?" Glenda rasped in her husky voice. She was sitting at Miss Baxter's vanity table holding up the silver-framed portrait of Miss Baxter in the pink dress. "Doesn't she look simply fabulous, Marla?"

"Oh yes," Marla replied from the back of the closet, "just like an Old Hollywood movie star. Isn't this what you've always wanted, sweetie?" Marla was rummaging through Miss Baxter's clothes, occasionally picking out a coat or dress, only to toss it carelessly on the floor.

"Yes—I mean, no," Louise stammered from the middle of the room.

"Well, what is it, darling, yes or no?" Glenda asked.

"Not like this! Not on the *Titanic*."

"Oh, that." Marla let out a low chuckle. "Details, details!"

"How do I get back?" Louise asked. "I don't want to be Miss Baxter anymore."

"How did you get here?" Glenda asked as she spritzed herself with some of Miss Baxter's fancy French perfume. It was starting to give Louise a massive headache, and she needed to keep on her toes.

"I don't know, you tell me. The last thing I remember I was putting on the dress in your store."

"Interesting," Marla purred. "I thought you said you wanted to try on that dress."

"As a matter of fact," Glenda interrupted, "she was quite demanding about it. Wasn't she, Marla?"

"Why, yes, I believe she was. We tried to warn you, sweetie, but you insisted."

"But it was only a dress," Louise began sobbing. "How was I supposed to know that all of this would happen? That I would end up stuck on a sinking ship! Does this concern you at all?"

"Only a dress," Glenda mimicked, powdering her face with the poofy white powder puff.

"Garments have a history of their own, my dear," Marla explained, tossing another chiffon gown on the floor. "We thought *you*, Louise, in particular, would have paid closer attention to what the fabric was trying to tell you."

"Fabric can't speak," Louise protested miserably, frustrated

that these strange women were speaking in riddles at a time like this.

"Oh, why does everyone take things so literally?" Glenda pontificated. "I personally would think twice before buying a tattered dress that smelled of seawater."

"Although the ocean breeze was quite lovely this afternoon," Marla said, fanning herself with a Japanese paper fan she had found in the steamer trunk. "I'm rather getting used to this sort of travel."

"Please help me get home. I never asked to be on a sinking ship. I miss my home. I miss who I was. Please." Louise was near tears. *Why is this happening to me?*

"Ah, isn't that sweet? Our fabulous starlet is homesick."

"I'm only a little girl," Louise begged. "I need my mom."

"Well, dear, you certainly don't look like *only a little girl* to me," Marla exclaimed in an exaggerated tone, lowering her glasses and carefully looking Louise over from head to toe.

"You would have a hard time convincing a jury of that one," Glenda added.

"But you know this isn't me. I'm not Miss Baxter! I saw you at the vintage sale...."

"Yes, yes, we hear you. It's just hard to feel sympathy when you look so darn gorgeous. What I wouldn't give for a figure like that." Glenda whistled. Both women started laughing.

Louise felt her eyes get watery. "You can have it," she cried.

"I want my old body back. I want my old life back. I was happy as Louise." And as soon as she said it, she knew it was true. She thought about her room with her canopy bed and her goldfish, Marlon, and her closet with its cozy reading nook, and she even longed for the familiar taste of her mom's infamous boiled, vinegary dinners. She needed to go home.

"Are you sure about that?"

"Yes, I've never been so sure of anything."

"It's not quite so simple, dear. We can't always get what we want, when we want it, can we?"

"Why did you pick me?" Louise asked.

"You found us, sweet pea," Glenda responded huskily.

"But why me? Why didn't Brooke get an invitation?"

"We saw that you understood the power of vintage. Some girls feel it, and some don't. We noticed the way you handled the fabric with respect, the way you felt the texture between your thumb and index finger. I don't think your friend has ever bought anything off the sale rack, let alone a vintage store. Although that didn't seem to stop her from showing up sans invitation!"

Louise laughed; that was true. She shook her head, snapping back to her new frightening reality.

"Are you witches?" she asked hesitantly. *Are Marla and Glenda magical? Is the dress?*

"Now, that's simply rude, dear. Didn't your mother teach

you any manners?" Marla asked curtly, trying on a floppy straw hat with a wink.

"Let's say we're stylists," Glenda said. "And we've worked with the best. You should be honored that we would even consider dressing you for a middle school dance."

"Honored? Look where that got me!" Louise yelped, looking around at her present surroundings. "It will be a miracle if I even make it to the dance."

"You'll make it to the dance, sweetie. We'll explain more once we know that we can trust you as one of our girls."

"Your girls?"

"Our Fashionistas. All in due time, my dear."

"Oh, look at the time," Marla exclaimed quickly, not looking at the time at all. "We really must be going."

"No! Please don't leave me!" Louise beckoned to them. "You still haven't told me how to get back to Connecticut."

"Haven't we, darling?" Glenda offered. "And haven't you already known all along?"

"Why can't you tell me?" Louise said. "You seem to have all the answers."

"Dear, that wouldn't be much fun, would it?" Glenda teased, getting up from the antique ivory vanity table. "You'll be amazed, sweet pea, that the littlest decisions of seemingly no importance, like what dress you wear to the party, end up being the decisions that change the course of your life forever."

And with that statement lingering in the air, the two women vanished from the room in a cloud of heavy perfume and purple smoke.

CHAPTER 34

Inhaling the lilac-scented remnants of her recently departed visitors, Louise felt a surge of intense panic; she was alone again. She picked up the sepia-toned photograph of Miss Baxter smiling in her pink dress. In a weird way, she knew she would miss being this glamorous lady. What if the power actually was embedded in the fabric of the dress? Could it have been that simple all along?

She heard a knock on the wardrobe door, and Anna entered. "Mr. Baxter asked that I check in on you," she said anxiously.

"Anna," Louise pleaded, grabbing her hand, "if I'm right, and the *Titanic* really does sink, promise me that you'll get on a lifeboat with as many passengers as you can. You must save yourself, since it seems I haven't been able to save any of us."

"I promise," Anna said shakily. They were both quiet for a moment. "Thank you."

"For what?" Louise asked. "I've really messed up. It doesn't seem like I've changed anything."

"I don't know," Anna said quietly, her eyes cast downward. "Believe it or not, today has been one of the most enjoyable in my life. I know you'd rather be in Connecticut, but I wish you could be the real Miss Baxter."

Louise blushed, caught off guard by Anna's heartfelt compliment. "Thank you, Anna." She gave her a warm hug. "You've been a great friend." Anna stiffened a bit when Louise wrapped her arms around her, still not used to Miss Baxter being so affectionate. "I know we just met each other a couple of days ago, but it seems like I've known you forever. I wish we could be friends in my other life," Louise added. She wished she could give Anna some present from the twenty-first century to remember her by, like an iPod with her favorite music or a great pair of skinny jeans.

"Me too," Anna said, beaming. "I'll be right back to help you to get dressed. Mr. Baxter will be waiting."

"Wait, Anna." Louise had an idea. "Have you told Christopher how you feel about him?" she asked, realizing that she could probably give Anna a few quick twenty-first-century dating tips. She was pretty good at giving advice to Brooke.

"Goodness, no. I couldn't do that," she replied, flustered.

"Of course you can. You're so old-fashioned!" exclaimed Louise. They both laughed at the slip. "Forget the rules. I mean he really helped us out today, and he could have gotten into a huge amount of trouble for doing that. He definitely likes you, a lot."

"I suppose that could be true," Anna surmised hesitantly.

"If you want a modern girl's perspective, I think if, I mean *when*, we get off this ship, you should invite him to see a play or have a picnic in the park."

"Me? Ask him?" Anna repeated, shocked.

"Totally," Louise replied confidently. "I mean, at this point what do you have to lose?" There was a moment of stunned silence.

"But what will I wear?" Anna finally asked. Louise laughed, the eternal female dilemma, even in the middle of a ship-sinking crisis.

"You should wear one of Miss Baxter's dresses," Louise suggested eagerly, combing through the closet for something that would look great on Anna.

"How about this turquoise one?" she asked, pulling out a stunning, long Grecian-style gown and holding it up to Anna so she could get a better look. "That's fabulous with your eyes." The aquamarine silk was the exact shade of Anna's blue-green eyes.

"I couldn't," Anna hesitated.

"Of course you can," Louise encouraged, pushing the dress on her. "We don't have much time—quickly, try it on. My

best friend and I used to share clothes all the time. It's like the best part of having girlfriends."

"If you insist," Anna agreed much less hesitantly. She pulled off her shapeless brown wool shift and slipped on the new dress over her old-fashioned undergarments. She looked amazing.

"That's hot," Louise squealed.

"Pardon?" Anna asked, looking alarmed.

"No, not hot. *Hot,*" Louise clarified. "It means you look, like, really unbelievably gorgeous."

"Thank you," Anna said with a blush.

"There's no way he's not going to fall madly in love with you in this dress. Check yourself out."

Anna walked over to the full-length mirror. A big smile spread across her face when she looked at herself in the gown.

"Told you so," Louise said, satisfied.

"Perhaps I can ask him to take an afternoon stroll...."

"Definitely!" Louise said as she handed Anna a matching pair of dyed bluish satin heels. Miss Baxter definitely knew how to accessorize.

"Ouch." Anna painfully tried to squeeze her feet into Miss Baxter's tiny shoes.

"Now take a spin down the catwalk. Like this," Louise said as she did her best attempt at a supermodel walk down the imaginary runway.

"Catwalk?" Giggling, despite the fact that she didn't know what a catwalk was, Anna copied her exaggerated hip swagger and strutted around in her new outfit.

"What's going on in here?" Mr. Baxter bellowed, pounding on the wardrobe door.

"Nothing, Uncle Baxter," Louise yelped quickly, not wanting him to walk in and interrupt the fashion show.

"Well, what's taking you so long? We're late for supper, and I'm famished!"

"Girl stuff," she replied, looking at Anna, alarmed at how much time must have passed.

"Women," Mr. Baxter said with a sigh from the other side of the closet door as he walked away.

The two girls exchanged a panicked look. Louise needed to come up with a plan and soon!

She looked at Anna for a long moment and felt a pang of something she could only describe as homesickness. Louise wanted to wrap her friend in the pink dress and keep them both safe and go back together to Connecticut. Maybe she could?

Anna quickly changed back into her old drab outfit and walked out of the dressing room to placate Mr. Baxter.

With her eyes closed, Louise imagined that she was back in her own walk-in closet and dreaming she was in another time. Except she knew that now, when she opened her eyes, it would be real. She thought once more of the other women who had worn her vintage clothes before her, about the previous lives of these garments, the way they connected her to the girls who lived before her, who went to their own dances and parties, who had their own dreams and boyfriends.

But what if the dress was only a dress? Louise couldn't imagine being Miss Baxter forever. She didn't want to drown. She knew that she needed to truly believe what Marla and Glenda told her about the power of vintage clothing, about listening to and respecting the energy of the fabric. "Louise, are you almost ready?" Anna's voice and timid knocking at the wardrobe door interrupted her reverie. "Mr. Baxter is getting rather irritable."

"Anna, come in here," Louise whispered urgently. "I think I've figured out how we can escape."

"Please, do tell!" Anna said eagerly, hurrying inside and shutting the ivory door behind her.

"Well, the last thing I remember doing before I ended up here was trying on the pink Lucile dress at a vintage sale."

"What is a vintage sale?" Anna asked, puzzled.

"I'll explain later—but this dress, Miss Baxter's dress, is the link. Maybe to get back, we just need to hold hands and put on the dress together. Do you want to check out what it's like almost one hundred years into the future?" She reached out her hand to Anna.

"Wait, where is Miss Baxter's pink dress?" Louise asked, frantically eyeing the wardrobe for any hint of that iridescent pink.

"I sent it down to be cleaned and pressed. It was a bit wrinkled after your fainting spell, and so I..." Anna said and then paused when she saw the horrified look on Louise's face.

"You mean the dress isn't here?"

"Well, it's not in the closet, but it is down with the cleaners. I'm sure it's fine. It's probably ready to be picked up by now."

"We need to find that dress!" Louise interrupted. "It's our only way off this boat!"

"You mean that dress is the link between Miss Baxter's life now and your life in the future?" Anna asked, trying to put the pieces together.

"Yes, I'm almost sure of it. Can you take me to the laundry room?"

Before Anna had a chance to answer, the boat made a sudden jolt. Louise heard a loud grinding noise, and then there was absolute quiet. The hum of the ship's engines had stopped. Everything was perfectly still and peaceful. And then the lights went out.

CHAPTER 35

"It's really happening!" Anna whispered into the still darkness.

"I guess I wasn't able to change anything," Louise replied in a sad and frightened voice.

"Who turned out the lights?" Mr. Baxter cried from the other room. "What the devil is going on here?" he cursed as he bumped into the furniture.

The electric lights sizzled and hissed, and within a few seconds, they flickered back on.

"We need to go help." The girls rushed out of the closet.

"Put your life jacket on!" Louise ordered Mr. Baxter, who was hopping around the bedroom holding his bruised toe.

"My God, does this mean you were right all along? It can't be," he whimpered, continuing his one-legged dance.

The girls opened the stateroom door and discovered the hallway was eerily deserted. Everyone seemed to have ignored the jolt, as though it were just a patch of choppy water.

Two crew members rushed past them down the empty corridor.

"What's happening?" Louise called after them.

"Everything is fine. Don't worry, ladies. But please return to your staterooms," one of them called over his shoulder. His voice was calm, but there was a look of terror on his clean-shaven face.

"We need to warn everyone," Louise declared. "Apparently we can't leave that job to the crew. They'll have everyone trapped in their staterooms until it's too late."

When the crew members were out of sight, Louise and Anna ran down the hallway, banging on stateroom doors.

"Everyone put on your life jackets! Get to the lifeboats! We've hit an iceberg!" they shouted.

Within seconds, doors began opening up and down the hallway. "What is the meaning of this commotion?" confused and angry passengers shouted at the girls.

A portly man, dressed only in a terrycloth bathrobe, half of his face still covered with foamy white cream, stepped out of his doorway and pointed his old-fashioned shaving razor at Louise. "Don't be absurd, the *Titanic* isn't sinking. There's not a drop of water anywhere," he said, pointing his razor down at the bone-dry carpet. "Now I intend to finish my shave," he said in a huff, slamming the door in their faces. Louise wondered how long it would take for the water to reach the first-class rooms; it would probably be too late at that point!

They ran to the next door. "You must be joking. It is scientifically impossible for this boat to sink," said a bespectacled man in the next cabin before slamming the door in their faces.

To her surprise, Lady Lucy Duff-Gordon opened the next door Louise pounded on.

"My dear, what in the heavens is the problem?"

Louise couldn't help but notice Lady Lucy was wearing a fabulous mauve silk kimono-style bathrobe with black piping, one of her signature designs.

"Lucile..."

"Please, doll, call me Lucy," she interrupted, holding her kimono closed.

"Okay, Lucy, the *Titanic* is going to sink, and as my dear friend, I am begging you to trust me on this one."

Lucy cocked her left eyebrow skeptically. "Don't you think we better wait for the captain to make that assessment?"

"Please, you are too talented to die. The world needs more Lucile designs," Louise pleaded earnestly.

She paused and looked deeply into Louise's eyes. "You're right. If we waited for men to call all the shots, we would all be at the bottom of the sea. And I did hear the most peculiar rumbling noise just now."

"Who's at the door?" Louise heard Sir Cosmo call from inside the stateroom.

"It's the first mate," Lady Duff-Gordon yelled into the room, winking at Louise. "Get your life jacket on, Cosmo, we're getting off early!"

She turned back toward Louise. "I should know better than to travel by sea, since I was almost shipwrecked as a child."

"Thank you for believing me and saving yourself," Louise said gratefully.

Lucy gave Louise a reassuring look and headed back into her room shouting, "Cosmo, get my squirrel coat—we're getting off this damn boat!"

Louise smiled with relief. Maybe she had just saved the life of one of her all-time favorite vintage designers. *How cool was that?*

With a renewed enthusiasm, she continued down the hall way, banging on the other closed doors. Unfortunately, the rest of the passengers were either already at dinner or ignoring her warnings.

"Go to the upper deck? I'll catch a chill, it's absolutely freezing tonight," answered a woman in a dressing gown, her face covered in a seaweed green face mask. *Slam.*

"It doesn't feel like we've hit anything. You women always overreact. Take a sedative!" a mustached man declared. *Slam.*

"This isn't working," Louise said helplessly to Anna. No one else wanted to believe that the slight jar they had felt earlier had actually had a serious impact. It seemed as though even Mr. Baxter had stayed in his stateroom. And it wasn't helping that the crew must have been hiding the full truth so no one would panic. Unless they also didn't realize how dire the situation was yet.

"I'll find Christopher on the upper deck. He'll alert the crew," Anna decided.

"Good idea. And I'll go down to the lower deck to find the dress. It's my only hope of getting back to my real life. I'll meet you on the upper deck as soon as I can."

In the stairwell, as Louise and Anna gave each other a quick hug before splitting up, Louise knew there was a chance she would never see her friend again. But they had to risk it.

CHAPTER 36

"Do you know where the laundry room is?" Louise asked a crew member who passed by her on the concrete narrow stairwell.

"Down the stairs, two flights, and then take a left, ma'am. But I would advise not going down there. Please return to your stateroom."

"What on earth for, has something happened?" Louise asked innocently, hoping someone would finally admit to what she already knew.

"No need for alarm, ma'am," he replied politely, completely avoiding the question. "But please return to your room and put on your life belt."

Louise ignored the officer and pushed her way past him downstairs. She didn't want to be placated; she wanted to hear someone finally start speaking the truth. Quickly making her way down two flights of stairs into a part of the ship she had never visited before, she opened the first door on her left and accidentally walked into what must have been a third-class cabin. The room was plainly furnished with two sets of wooden bunk beds, a simple oak desk and chair, and a white porcelain sink. It wasn't even as big as Miss Baxter's closet.

A mother was sitting on the edge of the bottom bunk in a white life jacket over a dark wool coat, zipping up the life jackets of her two children. Louise leaned against the doorway for balance; the rocking motion of the ship was much more pronounced down here.

"I'm sorry, I was looking for the laundry," Louise said.

The mother looked up, a thinly masked fear in her eyes. "Down the hall, take a left. You should find it three or four doors down."

"Thank you," Louise said.

"But, ma'am, I would recommend you go back up to your room. I'm not sure what's going on, but look." Just as she pointed down, Louise realized that ice-cold water was creeping over her feet. "We are going to wait here for instructions from the crew. You should probably do the same."

The ship was already taking on water. They must not have much time left!

"No, come with me." Louise knew that if the third-class passengers stayed in their rooms, they would never get off alive. "I'll take you to the upper deck. It's not safe down here."

The mother picked up one of the children and Louise the other.

Louise quickly walked them back the way she had come, knowing that to leave without finding the dress was taking a big risk, but she had to do it. If this woman was willing to listen, Louise had to save her.

"But how come you're not wearing a life vest?" the little boy in Louise's arms asked her as she adjusted him on her hip, and continued climbing the stairs.

"I'm still looking for mine," she replied, thinking that the pink evening dress would be a lot more helpful to her than any flotation device.

After three grueling flights of stairs, they made it up to the top deck. The air was bitter cold, and Louise clutched the shivering child tightly to her chest and looked out at a perfectly calm sea. The deck was still fairly deserted, and she immediately spotted Anna talking excitedly with Christopher across the way. Crew members were rushing by, but there still were only a small scattering of passengers by the lifeboats.

"Anna!" Louise cried, rushing over to her friend. "Will you please take care of them?" she asked, handing over the child in her arms. "The water has already started flooding the lower decks."

"Of course," Anna replied, taking the trembling boy in her arms.

"Follow me!" Christopher exclaimed. "You three will get to go for a ride in the little boats. Doesn't that sound fun?" he asked the kids, trying to keep them calm.

The kids nodded, wide-eyed. This was still like a game to them. They were too young to know to be scared.

Louise caught sight of Lady Lucy and Sir Cosmo, who were two of the first passengers on the upper deck. Lady Lucy was now wearing a sapphire blue head wrap and her long squirrel coat over her robe. Louise smiled at her pink satin slippers peeking out from under her fur. If Lucy Duff-Gordon was going down, she was definitely doing it in style. Even on the eve of a shipwreck, staring at this glamorous woman, Louise couldn't help but notice she was underdressed for the occasion.

"I need to go back down," Louise said as she turned back to Anna. "I still haven't found the dress."

"Be careful." Anna gave her another hug. "You were right. This is serious."

CHAPTER 37

Louise returned to the now-crowded stairwell. She was relieved to see that many of the passengers were finally wearing their bulky white life jackets on top of their overcoats and making their way up the concrete stairs with their families to the outer decks.

As Louise got lower into the belly of the boat, the water level began to rise. By the time she reached the bottom deck, it was rushing up to her knees. She once again took a left down the flooded corridor. She needed to find that dress.

She turned down another hallway and started trying the heavy brass door handles. A doorknob on her left pushed open, heavy with the rising water; she slipped in, shutting it behind her.

The electric lights were low and flickering, but still working. She had walked into what must have been the laundry room. Big, industrial, washing vats lined one wall, and hanging from the ceiling were racks and racks of clothes!

Louise began frantically searching the racks, pulling dresses and coats down into the water in the process. The laundry room was completely flooded now; hatboxes and button-up shoes bobbed by her legs. Clothes that she had yanked down were sticking to her calves like clingy pieces of seaweed. It was getting harder to wade through the knee-deep icy water. But where was her dress?

And then, in the dim, flickering light, Louise saw a blob of bubble gum pink float past, the skirt fanned out in a sweeping arc. The gold thread and tiny silver beads gave the dress a shimmering glow. In that moment, it really did look like it had magical qualities. Her fingers tingling with cold, she picked the dress up off of the icy skin of the water. She had found it. She pushed her way back through the now almost thigh-deep water, holding the soaking wet garment to her chest like a life preserver.

She hoped Anna was okay.

Louise waded out into the hallway, which was now overflowing with passengers trying to push their way to the exit.

"What's happening?" "Have we really hit an iceberg?" "Are we sinking?" Frantic questions were hurling through the air.

"Everyone stay calm! We need to get up to the lifeboats!" Louise shouted, trying to calm everyone down, feeling like a

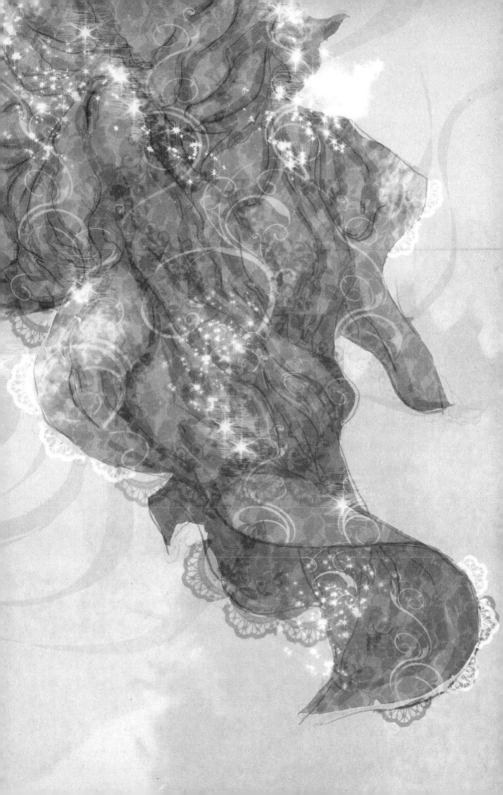

flight attendant on a crashing airplane. Her voice was drowned out by the cacophony. When she reached the stairwell, a cascade of bitterly cold seawater rushed toward her.

"Grab on to the railing," Louise directed some terrified passengers. "We need to make it upstairs! We can't turn back!" She held on tightly to the dress as she climbed up the staircase, grasping the slick wooden railing with all of her remaining strength.

Louise needed to make one more stop before she reached the upper deck. She wanted to make sure Mr. Baxter had not stayed in the room. She exited the stairs at the top floor, which was just starting to flood.

She once again started banging on the stateroom doors on her way to the Baxters' stateroom.

"What's happening? Is the *Titanic* going to sink?" Some of the passengers were still in their rooms, but clearly at this point they knew something was wrong.

"Yes, look!" Louise yelled, pointing down at the puddle of water soaking her feet. And then chaos broke out.

"We're going to sink! Help! Get to the lifeboats!" Within minutes, the hallway was filled with frantic first-class passengers wearing white life jackets over their furs and topcoats. There was a rush of people heading toward the exit stairwell at the end of the corridor, pushing to get to the upper deck. Louise continued to run down the halls, pounding on closed doors and making as much noise as she could to alert as many people as possible.

She ran against the sea of people, back to her stateroom. She tried the door handle. It wouldn't budge. She braced herself against the door and pushed her weight into it. The water created a strong resistance, as the level in the room had already reached her knees. The door slowly opened. Her calves numb with cold, Louise waded through the bedroom and sitting room. The framed photograph of Miss Baxter floated by her. Water had already seeped under the silver frame, and the image was blurry.

"Mr. Baxter?" Louise called into the adjoining room. She was relieved to find that the room was deserted. He must have listened to her and gone up to the deck by now! She left the room and pushed her way through the now panicking throngs to the stairs to get back upstairs. Now she needed to save herself.

Louise passed by the gymnasium that for once was completely filled with people. Hundreds of passengers were crowded inside trying to keep warm while they waited for a lifeboat. Some children were playing around on the camels and rowing machines. It made her sad that all T. W., the instructor, wanted was for people to come use his gym, and it took a collision with an iceberg to get them to finally show up.

The upper deck was complete pandemonium, set to music.

Louise was surprised and touched to see that, just like in the movie, the band from the first-class dining room had set up their instruments and were playing lively ragtime tunes as frantic passengers ran around trying to find their loved ones and get on lifeboats. The songs were strangely comforting.

"Anna!" Louise called out into the bitter cold, searching desperately for her friend among the swarms of people.

"Women and children only! Women and children, please load the lifeboats!"

Louise spun around to see First Officer Murdoch yelling directions to the panicked mob of people swarming the upper deck. She caught his eye for a moment. He shook his head in disbelief, perhaps realizing that she had been right all along, and then snapped back to reality and continued helping as many people as possible. "Women and children first, please! Stand back!"

Louise saw that Lucile and Cosmo were seated in the first boat that was being lowered down, three-quarters empty! Watching their jerky descent into the sea from across the deck, she felt a surge of anger and desperation course through her. She couldn't help but think of all the people who could be safe in that lifeboat. They must not have realized how precious every spot was.

"Anna!" Louise called again, the words coming out in cloudy puffs of frozen air.

Suddenly Mr. Baxter rushed by, with one crying child hoisted on each arm, and a sobbing woman following close behind. "Have no fear! I shall get you to a lifeboat!" he bellowed to the lady in his distinct baritone. Louise was going to wave to him but changed her mind, not wanting to distract him from helping this family. She called out for her friend instead.

"Anna!" Louise screamed.

She frantically searched the deck for her missing friend and instead spotted Mr. and Mrs. Straus, who were holding each other by the side of the boat. Crew members were pleading with Mrs. Straus to get into the lifeboat that was being lowered right next to them. T. W. McCawley was standing by the railing, handing off babies into the boat like an assembly line worker. His athletic prowess was certainly coming in handy.

"I will not leave my husband," Louise heard Mrs. Straus say firmly.

"Please, ma'am, get in the boat," one of the crew pleaded.

"Ida, get in. I will be fine," Mr. Straus begged, as at this point, only women and children were allowed in.

"We lived together, so we shall die together," Ida said in a tone that showed there was no changing her mind.

"Well, there is room for both of you. Please get in now. We need to lower this boat immediately."

"As long as there are women on this sinking ship, I will not save myself," Mr. Straus announced with fervor.

And with that statement, they walked together to a pair of deck chairs in the middle of all of the craziness and sat down quietly, holding hands beneath the star-speckled, moonless sky. Louise had never seen anything more courageous and beautiful.

Finally, she spotted Anna and Christopher across the deck. They were working together to try and fill up another boat. She watched Anna pick up a crying child and hand him off to his mother. Mrs. Astor was sitting in the same lifeboat, arms wrapped protectively across her pregnant belly, tears silently streaming down her face. Mr. Astor was nowhere to be seen.

Louise, wet and shivering, waved the pink dress above her head like a flag. Anna saw her and ran over.

"You found it!" Anna said as she hugged her soaking wet friend. "This is worse than I imagined." The ship pitched dangerously in one direction, and the girls grabbed on to each other for support as wooden deck chairs slid past them as if on roller skates.

"Look!" Anna pointed to a frantic Dr. Hastings clinging to the ropes of a lifeboat that was being hoisted up by the crew.

"Get me off this ship! I am a doctor!" he yelled as he grasped on for his life, feet kicking in the air, while the crew tried to grab his flailing limbs. A distress rocket shot up into the air with a bang and cascaded down like a shower of shooting stars.

"I'm sorry, but I can't leave Christopher. You're not supposed to be here, but I am. This is my time. I need to help," her friend cried as Louise lifted the dress above their heads.

"Anna, I'm not leaving! We're in this together." Louise shouted when the boat suddenly jackknifed and a collective scream pierced the night sky. Anna lost her balance and tumbled in the opposite direction with only a piece of the hem ripped off in her fingers.

Louise made a desperate cry for her friend before she herself fell backward onto the hard, splintered deck, as the dress came down on top of her, turning the starry night sky into a strawberry pink flash of color before everything went black once again.

"Vintage is a way of wearing history, a means by which we can turn the past into the present, even the future. Through us old fashion lives again."

HILARY ALEXANDER,
fashion director,
The Daily Telegraph

CHAPTER 38

"Open your eyes."

A woman's voice was calling to her from far away. Louise could not believe that she was having the same dream again. She didn't want to open her eyes this time. She decided to keep sleeping forever.

"Open your eyes," the melodic voice insisted.

There was something different about the voice this time, something warmly familiar. "Louise, please, open your eyes."

At the sound of her own name, Louise's eyes instinctively popped wide open.

"Mommy?"

Mr. and Mrs. Lambert were leaning over Louise, their foreheads creased with worry. Mrs. Lambert was stroking her face with her smooth hand. Her dad's blue-gray eyes were filled with concern.

"Sweetie? Oh, thank goodness. How are you feeling, my love?"

"Mommy?" Louise repeated in disbelief, so relieved and shocked to see her parents' faces. "Daddy? What...what happened?"

"I think your fever has finally broken," Mr. Lambert said warmly with a smile, dabbing a cool, damp washcloth on Louise's forehead. He was wearing his weekend casual outfit of khaki pants and a chambray blue button-down with the sleeves rolled up.

"Awesome!" a girl's voice called out from the other side of Louise's bedroom. Brooke jumped up from the rocking chair and walked over to Louise's bed.

"Brooke has been keeping you company," Mrs. Lambert explained.

Louise smiled at Brooke and felt a sudden wave of déjà vu. It was like she was looking at a younger version of Anna. "Thank you" was the only thing she could think to say.

"Whatever," Brooke said with a shrug. "We were really worried about you. I'm just glad you're finally awake. Besides, it wasn't like it was boring. Your mom was telling us the coolest stories about your great-aunt Alice."

"What about Aunt Alice?" Louise asked, sitting up in her bed.

"Like she was a gorgeous actress, and a first-class passenger on the *Titanic*! I mean, it's like a movie. I can't believe you've never told me about her."

"She was?" Louise asked, trying to put all the pieces together. She was beginning to feel like Dorothy waking up in Kansas after her trip to the Land of Oz.

"Yes, dahling. I told you and Brooke the story of Alice's adventures on the high seas when you were drifting in and out of this fever," she explained.

"Why hadn't you told me before?" Louise asked, confused, thinking back to that oil portrait hanging in their dining room of her elderly great-aunt.

"I heard the whole story for the first time last week when I was in London. Alice's daughter didn't start talking about it until she was on her deathbed. Her mother was a very private person. I'll be sure to tell you the story again one day."

"What happened to me?" Louise asked.

"You fainted at that vintage sale, which you insisted on going to," Mrs. Lambert said, making a *tsk* noise, not quite able to mask the I-told-you-so tone of her voice. "Brooke and these two nice ladies brought you home."

"Marla and Glenda?" Louise asked.

"Yes, it was us."

Louise let out a startled gasp. Marla was perched up at the edge of Louise's oak wooden dresser like a cat. She hadn't noticed her before.

"Wow." Louise shook her head in disbelief. *"You are real."*

"Of course they are real," her mom said, glancing at Louise with concern.

Glenda was leaning against the wall next to Marla, her imposing height seeming even more dramatic from Louise's bed. Had she been there a moment ago?

"Well now, my dear Mrs. Lambert, we told you she'd pull through," Glenda cooed, giving Louise a pat on the head.

"But why did I faint?" Louise asked, as none of this was making any sense.

"Dr. Jacobs thinks it may have been food poisoning. Such a high fever, sudden upset stomach... Do you remember eating anything unusual before you got sick?" her dad asked.

Louise thought back to the mysterious, crusty crab dip she sampled at the vintage sale and felt her stomach turn over.

"Yes..." She felt nauseous again at the thought of it. "It must have been the crab dip."

"Well, let's not jump to any conclusions," Marla interjected, jumping off the dresser with surprising agility.

Mrs. Lambert shook her head disapprovingly. "Bad mayonnaise. That would never happen with vinegar. I've never trusted mayonnaise. And that gelatinous texture..."

"Can we not talk about this now?" Louise asked, clutching her stomach.

"Gross," Brooke said. "Let's start a club against mayonnaise. You can be the president, Louise." They all laughed. Well, with two notable exceptions.

"Did I miss the dance?" Louise asked, suddenly remembering the semiformal with disappointment.

"Don't worry, dear, the dance isn't for a few days. You've only been with this fever for a couple of hours now. Although the semiformal may have to be postponed," Mrs. Lambert added, adjusting the washcloth.

"Yeah, it was so crazy. There was a water main break in the school gymnasium. The whole place is flooded," Brooke explained.

Louise heard Marla—or was it Glenda?—chuckle under her breath.

"I think we did manage to find you just the right ensemble," Marla said, satisfied.

Louise gasped. The carnation pink Lucile dress that she had tried on in the store, the same one she had dreamed she was wearing on the *Titanic*, was hanging on the front of her closet door, now a little wrinkled but dry, and with that same noticeable rip in the hem.

"Ummm, I think I might wear something else," she stammered.

"Nonsense," Glenda chimed in. "Trust yourself in our

capable hands. You'll make it to the Fairview Junior High School dance. That is, if that's where your heart truly wants to take you."

"Oh, it is, I swear," Louise said with a smile. For once, there was no place she would rather be.

"That's what we thought." Glenda winked at her.

"Do you know if Todd is going with anyone?" Louise asked Brooke, trying to sound nonchalant. "I mean, not that he'd even want to talk to me at this point."

"Well, you'd think that after you ran away from him the other day in front of the whole seventh grade, he would have asked someone else," Brooke said, suppressing a smile. "But apparently you're the only one on his list. I'm pretty sure he's going by himself."

Louise grinned with relief. "I think I made a mistake about something."

Brooke raised a perfectly plucked eyebrow. "By the way, you were right. Kip finally asked me."

Louise laughed. The universe was back to normal.

"Well, we must be off. I hope you have a wonderful time at the dance, my dear. You've most certainly earned it. Come see us again sometime soon," Glenda said. And with these words, Marla and Glenda were out of the room in a flash.

"Very peculiar ladies, I must say," Mrs. Lambert said, shaking her head. "Well, Brooke, I'm sure your parents would love to have you home. And Louise should get some sleep. I'll be right back with some tea and buttery toast with raspberry jam. In the meantime, there's water and juice on the bedside table."

"Glad to see you're feeling better, chicken," her dad said as he ruffled her hair. She smiled, happy to be called anything but Miss Baxter, even "chicken." "I have a deposition I need to prepare for, but I'll go into the office a little late and see you in the morning. Get some rest."

Mr. and Mrs. Lambert both gave their daughter a kiss on the cheek, and they all left the room together, leaving Louise alone, snuggled under her grandmother's patchwork quilt, exhausted, and for the moment, perfectly and utterly content.

She glanced over at the dress hanging on the door and smiled. What an amazingly fun and terrifying and sad dream she'd had. She wondered if all of her vintage clothes had such profound histories attached to them.

As Louise reached over to her nightstand to get a sip of water, she saw a pale teal envelope propped up against her clock radio.

With a nervous curiosity, she picked up the envelope that had her name written on it in the now familiar script.

To: Ms. Louise Lambert

She turned it over shakily and saw the iconic bloodred wax seal.

Mrs. Lambert knocked twice on the bedroom door and, without waiting for Louise to answer, entered carrying a silver tray with a steaming hot teacup and a pile of toast. Quickly, Louise placed the envelope in her night table under her diary. She shut the drawer and gave her mom a reassuring smile as she leaned back on her pillow.

CHAPTER 39

Every time she shut her eyes, Louise could feel the waves rocking her bed like a lifeboat tossed in a choppy sea. It was almost 2:30 AM, and she was afraid to fall asleep and find herself back on the *Titanic*. Finally she accepted the fact that she would not be able to sleep and switched on her bedside lamp. Shivering, she sat up in bed and wrapped her arms around her knees. She couldn't ignore the feeling in her gut that it was real. That it hadn't all been just a dream, a hallucination brought on by food poisoning. The experience was too vivid.

The house was dark and quiet as Louise wrapped herself up in her grandmother's quilt and walked over to her computer. She needed to find out the real story of the *Titanic*. The computer woke up with a soft hum, and Louise signed on, typed in "*Titanic* Disaster," and began her clandestine research.

THE RMS *TITANIC* WAS AN OLYMPIC-CLASS PASSENGER LINER THAT BECAME INFAMOUS FOR HER COLLISION WITH AN ICEBERG AND DRAMATIC SINKING ON APRIL 15, 1912. THE *TITANIC* WAS THE LARGEST PASSENGER STEAMSHIP IN THE WORLD AT THE TIME OF HER SINKING. CAPTAIN EDWARD JOHN SMITH, 62, WAS THE CAPTAIN OF THE IMPRESSIVE VESSEL. SHE WAS CONSIDERED A PINNACLE OF NAVAL ARCHITECTURE AND TECHNOLOGICAL ACHIEVEMENT, AND WAS THOUGHT BY MANY TO BE "PRACTICALLY UNSINKABLE." DURING THE *TITANIC*'S MAIDEN VOYAGE (FROM SOUTHAMPTON, ENGLAND; TO CHERBOURG, FRANCE; QUEENSTOWN, IRELAND; THEN NEW YORK) SHE STRUCK AN ICEBERG AND SANK MERELY A FEW HOURS LATER, HAVING BROKEN INTO TWO PIECES AT THE AFT EXPANSION JOINT.

FOR HER TIME, THE *TITANIC* WAS SECOND TO NONE IN HER LAVISH COMFORT AND EXTRAVAGANCE. SHE WAS THE FIRST SHIP TO OFFER A HEATED SALTWATER SWIMMING POOL, STATE-OF-THE-ART GYMNASIUM, LIBRARIES FOR EACH PASSENGER CLASS, AND AN ELEGANT FIRST-CLASS DINING ROOM THAT OFFERED SUPERB FOUR-STAR CUISINE. THE CROWN JEWEL OF THE SHIP'S INTERIOR WAS UNDOUBTEDLY THE GRAND STAIRCASE. EXTENDING DOWN TO E DECK AND DECO-

RATED WITH OAK PANELING AND GILDED BALUS-
TRADES, IT WAS TOPPED BY AN ORNATE WROUGHT-
IRON-AND-GLASS DOME, WHICH BROUGHT IN NATURAL
LIGHT.

THE FIRST-CLASS PASSENGER LIST FOR *TITANIC'S*
MAIDEN VOYAGE INCLUDED SOME OF THE RICHEST AND
MOST PROMINENT PEOPLE IN THE WORLD. AMONG THEM
WERE MILLIONAIRE JOHN JACOB ASTOR IV AND HIS
WIFE, MADELEINE; INDUSTRIALIST BENJAMIN
GUGGENHEIM; MACY'S DEPARTMENT STORE OWNER
ISIDOR STRAUS AND HIS WIFE, IDA; FASHION DESIGNER
LADY LUCY DUFF-GORDON AND HER HUSBAND AND
BUSINESS PARTNER, SIR COSMO DUFF-GORDON; FLAM-
BOYANT MANAGER AND PRODUCER HENRY BAXTER AND
HIS NIECE AND PROTÉGÉ, ENGLISH SILENT FILM STAR
ALICE BAXTER....

Louise was stunned. "Oh my goodness," she whispered.
"Everything really did happen. And this has to be my great
aunt Alice. This must have been the story Mom was trying to
tell me."

She *did* exist. The next question that popped into Louise's
head was one she wasn't sure she wanted to know the answer
to, but she had to. Did Mr. Baxter survive? Did Anna? With a

sweaty palm, Louise gripped the mouse and scrolled slowly down the page.

On the night of April 14, the *Titanic* struck an iceberg and sank three hours later on April 15, 1912, with great loss of life. The United States Senate investigation reported that 1,517 people perished in the accident.

Heart pounding, Louise went back and typed in "*Titanic*: List of Dead." Within seconds, there it was, in the public archives, a list of everyone who died that night. With each name that she read, Louise felt a constricting in her chest that tightened as she went down the list: J. J. Astor, Ida and Isidor Straus, Captain Smith.... She could picture some of them so clearly. This would never be a list of faceless names to her. The *Titanic* was no longer a glamorous, cinematic background— for the first time in her life, history was real to her, because now so were its people. Louise had almost made it through the whole list when she came across the name she was dreading to find. She hadn't been able to save him after all.

She clicked her mouse on Mr. Baxter's name.

It was said that Mr. Henry Baxter and Mr. Benjamin Guggenheim put on their best suits,

POURED THEMSELVES GLASSES OF THEIR FINEST SCOTCH, AND WENT DOWN TO THE SMOKING ROOM TO DIE LIKE GENTLEMEN. ACCORDING TO HIS BEREAVED NIECE, ALICE, HER UNCLE AND MR. GUGGENHEIM REFUSED TO TAKE A SEAT ON THE LIFEBOATS WHEN THEY KNEW THAT THERE WERE NOT ENOUGH SEATS FOR EVERY WOMAN AND CHILD. IN THE ONLY INTERVIEW ALICE HAS GIVEN ABOUT THE DISASTER, SHE TOLD THE *HERALD TRIBUNE*, "HE WAS MY UNCLE, MY MANAGER, AND MY DEAREST FRIEND. HE WAS A TRUE GENTLEMAN, AND WE WILL ALL MISS HIM DEEPLY. IT IS TOO PAINFUL TO REMEMBER THAT NIGHT. I MUST HAVE BLOCKED IT OUT OF MY MEMORY, FOR I HAVE ONLY A FOGGY RECOLLECTION OF ANYTHING THAT OCCURRED ON BOARD THAT SHIP, BUT I WILL DO MY BEST TO CARRY ON."

Louise opened up a new window and typed in *"Titanic Survivor Stories."* She clicked on the first link.

LADY LUCY DUFF-GORDON AND SIR COSMO DUFF GORDON BOARDED THE *TITANIC* AT CHERBOURG, FRANCE, UNDER THE ASSUMED NAMES MR. AND MRS. MORGAN, SO AS NOT TO ATTRACT UNWANTED MEDIA ATTENTION UPON ARRIVAL IN NEW YORK CITY. ON THE EVE OF THE DISASTER, THEY ESCAPED IN LIFEBOAT 1, NOW INFA-

MOUSLY DUBBED "THE MILLIONAIRE'S BOAT," WITH
THEIR SECRETARY, LAURA MABEL FRANCATELLI, AND
NINE OTHERS, MOST OF THEM CREWMEN. THE BOAT WAS
DESIGNED TO HOLD FORTY PASSENGERS.

THERE HAS BEEN MUCH SPECULATION AS TO WHETHER
SIR COSMO BRIBED THE CREW NOT TO TURN BACK AND
RESCUE THE OTHERS, IN FEAR THAT THE BOAT WOULD
BE MOBBED. IN FACT, IT HAS BEEN CONFIRMED THAT HE
DID WRITE CHECKS TO ALL OF THE CREW WITH HIM,
BUT HE CLAIMS IT WAS A GOODWILL GESTURE TO HELP
TIDE THEM OVER UNTIL THEIR NEXT ASSIGNMENT. A
DISGUSTED CREW MEMBER ALSO ON BOARD LIFEBOAT I
RECALLS LADY DUFF-GORDON, IN THE MIDST OF THE
MOST DEADLY AND HORRIFIC SEA DISASTER IN RECENT
HISTORY, COMMENTED TO HER SECRETARY, "THERE IS
YOUR BEAUTIFUL NIGHTDRESS, GONE."

Louise clicked on the next link with a dread-filled
anticipation.

MANY PASSENGERS ON BOARD THE *TITANIC* REFUSED TO
TALK ABOUT THEIR EXPERIENCES. IT WASN'T UNTIL
MANY YEARS LATER, SOME NOT UNTIL THEY WERE ON
THEIR DEATHBEDS, THAT THEIR STORIES CAME TO

LIGHT. BUT ALTHOUGH THE *TITANIC* IS ONE OF HISTO-
RY'S MOST INFAMOUS SEA TRAGEDIES, IT ALSO HELD
MANY STORIES OF GREAT HEROISM AND BROUGHT FORTH
SOME TERRIFIC TALES SHOWCASING THE BRAVE AND
ALTRUISTIC NATURE OF THE HUMAN SPIRIT.

Wide-eyed, Louise scanned the page, stopping suddenly
at her friend's name:

ANNA HARD, THE SEVENTEEN-YEAR-OLD MAID OF FIRST-
CLASS PASSENGER MISS ALICE BAXTER, WAS SOMEONE
WHO TURNED INTO THE DEFINITION OF A TRUE HERO-
INE, RISKING HER OWN LIFE TO SAVE THE LIVES OF OTH-
ERS. IN AN INTERVIEW SHE GAVE TO THE *HERALD
TRIBUNE* SHORTLY AFTER RETURNING HOME TO ENG-
LAND FOLLOWING THE DISASTER, MISS HARD, WHO
WOULD LATER BECOME MRS. BRADY, AS SHE LATER
MARRIED MR. CHRISTOPHER BRADY OF THE *TITANIC*
CREW, SAID THAT SHE WAS ABLE TO KEEP CALM AND
TAKE CHARGE WHILE EVERYONE ELSE WAS PANICKING
BECAUSE SHE HAD A PREMONITION THAT SUCH A DISAS
TER WOULD TAKE PLACE. SHE WAS ABLE TO ASSIST THE
MEN IN FILLING SEVERAL LIFEBOATS TO CAPACITY WITH
WOMEN AND CHILDREN, WHILE ELSEWHERE ON THE
SHIP, HALF-FILLED BOATS WERE BEING LOWERED BY

TERRIFIED CREW MEMBERS WHO FAILED TO REALIZE THEIR FATAL ERROR. THEY DIDN'T FULLY COMPREHEND THE GRAVITY OF THE SITUATION, THAT THE "UNSINKABLE" SHIP WAS, IN FACT, SINKING, THAT EACH EMPTY SEAT ON THE LIFEBOAT SIGNIFIED ONE PERSON WHO WOULD BE LEFT TO GO DOWN WITH THE RMS TITANIC. MISS HARD RELUCTANTLY GOT ONTO ONE OF THE LAST LIFE-BOATS ALONG WITH MISS BAXTER BUT LAMENTS THAT SHE WAS NOT ABLE TO TAKE MORE PEOPLE WITH HER, EVEN THOUGH, ACCORDING TO HER WORDS, SHE "FELT INEVITABLY THIS WAS COMING."

Teary-eyed, Louise smiled proudly at the account of Anna's bravery. Anna wasn't going to become an old maid after all! She typed in "Anna Hard, Christopher Brady wedding," and an announcement from the *London Times* popped up on her screen.

MISS ANNA HARD, 17, AND MR. CHRISTOPHER BRADY, 19, WERE MARRIED THIS SUNDAY AT GRACE COURT CHURCH. THE COUPLE MET UNDER EXTRAORDINARY CIRCUMSTANCES WHEN THEY WERE WORKING ON BOARD THE *TITANIC* ON ITS ILL-FATED MAIDEN VOYAGE. SHE WAS THE PERSONAL MAID OF ACTRESS MISS ALICE BAXTER, AND HE SERVED AS A QUARTERMASTER UNDER

Captain Smith. It was reported that they both saved many lives that evening, helping others into the safety of the lifeboats. Mr. Brady took charge of one of the final lifeboats, with Miss Hard and Miss Baxter on board, rowing it to safety, deftly avoiding the deadly whirlpool that was created when the broken ship finally sunk. "She was convinced the *Titanic* was doomed all along," Mr. Brady told our reporter. "The next time my wife has a premonition, you bet I'm going to listen!"

What if she, Louise, had somehow affected the past? Maybe she *had* been able to make a little bit of difference after all!

Louise began clicking through various pictures, now all oddly familiar to her. drawings and sketches of the exterior of the ship, the Grand Staircase, the gymnasium with its mechanical camels, a few stills of the Kate Winslet and Leonardo DiCaprio movie, and finally she came to a black-and-white newspaper photograph. The grainy photo was a group shot of some fancily dressed people holding raised champagne glasses and standing in front of enormous smokestacks with White Star Line painted in block lettering on the funnels. Louise zoomed in. It was Mr. and Mrs. Astor, and Ida and Isidor

Straus! And, could it be? She clicked the magnifying glass again, focusing in on the girl who was third from the left. She let out a cry of surprise—this girl in the photograph was most definitely *her*!

Louise scanned down to read the caption. April 12, 1912, RMS *Titanic*, A Deck. From Left: Jacob and Madeleine Astor, unidentified first-class female passenger, Ida and Isidor Straus... *Ohmigod*. Louise zoomed in even more until the image began to get pixilated. It was undeniably her—same eyes, same nose, same frizzy hair, and tight-lipped smile. She was the unidentified female passenger. She was really there! And now she had proof.

Louise picked up the pink dress gingerly, with a newfound respect for its history. She hung it at the front of the closeted clothing rack. It was by far the oldest piece in her vintage collection.

She suddenly remembered the lavender envelope she had hidden in her nightstand. It was still under her leather-bound diary, just where she had left it. With a fluttery excitement tickling her stomach, she broke open the wax seal and extracted the thick stationery.

She eagerly pulled out a handwritten note in a flowery red script.

Dearest Louise,

Darling, you looked absolutely fabulous in your pink dress!

Louise could almost hear Glenda's raspy voice speak through the pages. Squinting, she held the letter up to the light and started reading.

We hope you will continue to be part of our small, select group of very important clients. We want to pass on a bit of our wisdom about the importance of vintage clothing to you, our newest Fashionista. It takes a special kind of person to realize that when you wear vintage you are carrying a bit of the past on your body, and the possibility that vintage can have an impact on your modern life. But there's also the responsibility that comes with this privilege of owning a piece of the past.

When someone has a strong spirit, their energy never disappears. It takes another form and gets scattered throughout the atmosphere and embedded in the things and places that were most intimate and important to them. And it takes a certain type of sensitivity to pick it up. It is no wonder that women have clothing that carries a bit of their spirits with them. This is especially true if a very traumatic or wonderful event happened while she was wearing that garment. Someone's soul can't die; it simply gets transformed and transmuted.

That's why vintage clothing is so powerful. You've felt it before, we know.

Unfortunately, my dear, we are now living in a time where we want fast and cheap and modern. True Fashionistas do not shop at the mall!

Don't forget your history, Louise. If we do, we are destined to repeat the past, as though for the first time, without benefiting from any of the knowledge that can be gained from those who have come before us.

In the words of the inimitable French designer Coco Chanel, "Fashion fades, only style remains the same."

Welcome to the club, my darling. Remember, you are already a star. Now it's time to dress like one!

Marla and Glenda

Louise put down the letter, trying to take it all in. "Are you a stylist or a philosopher?" she whispered into her empty bedroom.

"What's the difference?" She could have sworn she heard Glenda rasp from the ether.

Louise reached back into the envelope and pulled out a smaller card.

She smiled, exposing a mouthful of metal. Brooke's thirteenth birthday was only three weeks away, and Louise knew exactly where she would find the perfect party dress.

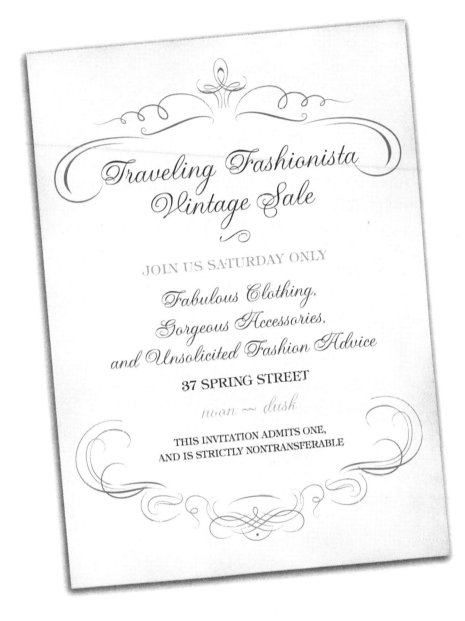

Traveling Fashionista Vintage Sale

JOIN US SATURDAY ONLY

*Fabulous Clothing,
Gorgeous Accessories,
and Unsolicited Fashion Advice*

37 SPRING STREET

noon ~ dusk

THIS INVITATION ADMITS ONE,
AND IS STRICTLY NONTRANSFERABLE

ACKNOWLEDGMENTS

My deepest gratitude to my parents, whose lifelong encouragement and love has made this book (and everything else) possible. To the brilliant and understated Robert Josovitz for sparking the conversation when I showed up for brunch one morning in Mrs. Baxter's white wool coat; that was the day when everything shifted for me. To Julian Schnabel for teaching a girl from Connecticut a thing or two about art, life, and generosity, and for showing through his inimitable example that other worlds are possible. Thanks to Alex Fuller Braden for his pro bono expertise. Two tickets to the premiere are in the mail. Thank you to Nancy Shea and Todd Lyon at the New Haven Fashionista store for inspiring the imaginations and inner divas of so many lucky customers. This book, and my personal vintage collection, would not be the same without you.

My most sincere thanks to the honorary Traveling Fashionistas: my fabulous agent, Elisabeth Weed, and editor extraordinaire, Cindy Eagan. Elisabeth, I will always be grateful for your early support. Your humor and blind optimism made this long journey a blast, and thank you for connecting me with Cindy, my soul mate of editors. I feel unbelievably lucky to have you two on my side. Thank you.